KALEIDOSCOPE OF SHORT STORIES

Julie Taylor Timms

jmtimms@hotmail.com

Cover illustrated by

Kelsey Vanraay

INDEX OF STORIES

1   A Feather Present …………….. Page 8

2   A Letter of Apology ….……. Page 11

3   Aggie …………………. Page 14

4   An Awesome Oddity .………. Page 19

5   Banking Your Assets ………. Page 24

6   Barbara Ann Scott …………. Page 27

7   Barefoot Memory …………. Page 31

8   Before Television ……………. Page 39

9   Bippity Boppity Boo …………. Page 44

10   Boating Accident Rescue …… Page 49

11   Boom Town Fort McMurray … Page 56

12   Bucket List …………………… Page 62

13	Canada Day At Lakeview Park ...	Page 65
14	Casey	Page 69
15	Continental Turbans At The Ex ...	Page 74
16	Decorating Disasters Of The 70's ..	Page 78
17	Demolition Derby	Page 87
18	Evading The Blues	Page 95
19	Eye Contact	Page 99
20	Failed Attempts At Mothering ...	Page 102
21	Family Positions	Page 106
22	Fight Or Flight	Page 110
23	Food And Me	Page 113
24	Forgetfully Yours	Page 116
25	Frazer Canyon Run Away	Page 123
26	Fred's Inheritance	Page 129

27	An Unsung Hero	Page 132
28	Grandma's Photo	Page 135
29	Harry Taylor's Childhood	Page 139
30	Helping Jaunita Move	Page 142
31	Hettie's Journal	Page 145
32	If I Were A Gem Stone	Page 149
33	Julie's Dreams	Page 151
34	Lack Of Fashion Sense	Page 155
35	Less Is More	Page 159
36	Letter Of Resignation	Page 161
37	Lie Or Not	Page 164
38	Lipstick In The Pocket	Page 167
39	My Amazing Cousin	Page 174
40	My Fears And Idiosyncrasies	Page 179

41 My Mother's Famous Words ..... Page 182

42 My Parents Sacrifice ....Page 186

43 My Pets Dislikes .... Page 190

44 Our Wedding Day .... Page 193

45 Ornery Cuss .... Page 196

46 Out Of My Comfort Zone ....Page 199

47 Pigs And Pears .... Page 204

48 Pinocchio's Love Affair With Jill . Page 205

49 Remembrance Day .... Page 211

50 Shannon's Intuition ....Page 215

51 Soup Kitchen ....Page 220

54. The Black Donnellys Massacre And Curse
.... Page 231

52 Tent Revival Meeting ……….... Page 235

53 The Apple Never Falls Far From The Tree
…………………………………………...Page 239

55 The House Fire And The Button Hook Boot
……………………………………… Page 243

56 The Fire Storm ……………… Page 248

57 The Life Of A Tree ………… Page 252

58 The Princess Dress ………… Page 254

59 The Roller Coaster Ride ……… Page 257

60 The Shiny Red Tool Box ……… Page 261

61 The Things I Gave Up During My Life
…………………………………………...Page 266

62 Thrift Store Parking Lot ……… Page 270

63 Trailer Park Tacky …………… Page 274

64 Twelve Months Of Heather … Page 277

65 Unmatched Luggage .... Page 279

66 Victorian Ways .... Page 284

67 Wisdom .... Page 287

68 Bibliography .... Page 290

A FEATHER PRESENT

Some folks believe that the spirit of their deceased loved ones can revisit them in other forms such as, butterflies, birds or other objects. Dreaming of the departed is the most common way I have of reuniting with them. Others though, use metaphoric items such as coins or feathers to reinstate their belief in the worldly presence of their departed. I encountered both a dream and a feather in my super natural experience.

It all began when I decided to rewrite the stories I had written for my grandchildren and great grandchildren over a period of twenty odd years. The stories were fictional but based on them, a dog named Knee-high and me, their Grandmother. They were cute stories, but something was missing. They needed a villin to be exciting. Everyone loves to see a villin act out the parts of life that we all have to contend with, like bad behavior, jealousy and plotting to get another in trouble. Kids understand that stuff. They eat it up.

To satisfy that need I resurrected our pretty little budgie bird named Two-bits. He came to life again with plenty of his true attitude intact. He spiced up the stories with his naughty behaviour, cheeky ways and compulsion to bite little fingers that poked at him. I truly enjoyed reminiscing of the days when the budgie, the dog and the kids filled my life with love and laughter.

The books were printed and given out as Christmas gifts but that was not the end of this story. One cold January night I dreamt that Two-bits came to visit me. He was as happy to see me as I was to see him. He was bigger than I remembered, I thought, as I held him on my finger and kissed his breast the way I used to all those years ago.

He opened his wings and encircled my head in a hug while his beak rested on my nose. It was such a beautiful moment. I was enchanted by our love for each other. I am certain it was his way of thanking me for writing him into the stories. But that was not all there was to it.

The next morning on my way to the bathroom, I noticed a tail feather in the hall just outside my bedroom door. This was the middle of winter. Birds were seldom heard or seen. The hall has no window. Even if one of the screened windows in a bedroom was open, which it was not on a 20 below zero, windy January night, how did the feather get there. The only explanation I could come up with was the feather was a gift from Two-bits. It was verification that the bounds of love go on beyond this plane not just for humans but for the animals that touch our hearts too.

    I placed the feather in the arms of an angle in my china cabinet where it can be a constant reminder that love never dies. I don't have all the answers to the spiritual or psychic wonders in our universe. I just know that there is more to it all than most of us understand.

A LETTER OF APOLOGY

Dear Fred,

Although you passed away over 20 years ago, I would like to express my regret for not recognizing all the things I took for granted in our relationship. Let me begin with the first day I saw you. I had no idea that the wink you gave me and the one I returned to you would be the beginning of a friendship that would last over forty years.

Nor did I recognize that our love for each other would produce five beautiful children, take us down many different paths and introduce us to more pleasure, passion and illusive dreams than either of us could have imagined. There were times when I thought your pipe dreams were unrealistic, but you didn't listen to me very often, thank goodness. I lacked your vision and your courage to try something different. I'm sorry I opposed and stifled most of your crazy get rich schemes.

I will admit there were times when I doubted we would make it over all the rough spots and financial hardships we suffered, due to our immaturity and lack of education, but we carried on. We had no other choice. There was no one else able to shoulder our responsibilities while we matured. I apologize for blaming you for the hardships we endured before I was able to join you on the work force. Those were the years you said you felt like a father bird returning to the nest but never able to bring home enough to satisfy our growing family's needs.

    I'm sorry I took for granted all the fun we had sharing the comedy of the daily events that unfolded around us. Our lives were so rich with laughter, friendships, good times, music and happiness; I never thought it would end. And when it did I became aware of just how much I had taken for granted.

    All those times I accused you of not doing much around the house were retracted after you passed away and I had to look after things I never had to take care of before, like changing blown fuses, fueling the lawn mower, or turning off the outside water supply in the fall. I apologize for not giving you more credit for taking care of those chores that then became my responsibility.

Thinking back, I also realize, I never made life easy for you when my hormones made me fall victim to the poor me syndrome that I suffered often, tears and all. There were other times when I gave you the cold shoulder because I was angry and expected you to damn well know why, but you seldom had a clue.

I gave you lots of advice, whether you asked for it or not, on your driving ability, your choice in clothing, your personal hygiene and how much alcohol you should consume when at a party.

I apologize for all the above and can't wait to get to Heaven to tell you how you always gave me enough to bitch about to keep me happy and I miss you just as much today as the day you passed away, July 18, 1997.

Your loving wife, Julie.

AGGIE

How can I possibly put 46 years of friendship with Aggie into a dozen or so paragraphs? I'd need to write a full-length book to cover all the shenanigans and great times we had together. Some would call it comical fiction while others may find parts that came close to being X rated. Sharing a friendship with Aggie was always fun and never dull or boring. It held far more laughter than tears.

Aggie loved music and although she never played an instrument or sang on key, she hosted some of the best jam sessions at her home in Oshawa. And after we moved out of town, it was our house the guitar picking, banjo strumming, fiddle playing musicians gathered at, whether-or-not we were home. They would allow me to be in the band too. playing the spoons occasionally.

Shortly after we met Aggie, Fred's old pickup truck got rear ended by a concrete truck at a red light. This is when we discovered what a good artist Aggie was. She re-lettered the name on the front hood from Skinny Minnie to Saggy Maggy. She went on from there to take folk art painting classes and adorned all sorts of treasures her husband, Gord made in his workshop. I have several of those pieces in my homes.

Another thing Aggie was excellent at was putting out a delicious and plentiful meal. She spoilt us with her savoury cooking and home baking. I remember her famous pea soup that was part of our traditional meal fare on the house boat. You can imagine all the putting along we were doing while anchored and playing cards in the cabin of that tiny boat.

After they moved back to Aggie's home town of Deep River and bought a chip truck, they became known as having the best fries in town. That money -making business generated enough profit for them to enjoy staying in Florida all winter.

While visiting them there, one winter, Aggie got caught swiping an orange from a tree along the edge of someone's property. She talked her way out of it as only she could. Being so short had some advantages. She told the trooper she was too short to reach the branches and the orange in her hand came from the ground. She got away with it, too.

Aggie and I looked like the odd couple where ever we went. She was so short and nimble and I so big and clumsy, but we did have some things in common. We both liked Cherry whiskey and getting up at the crack of dawn.

Coming from the small northern town of Deep River, Aggie had never ridden on a roller-coaster. I decided to remedy that calamity one summer at Marine Land where the coaster did two upsides down loops. We gave Fred and Gord our purses to hold while she and I made our maiden voyage on an upside down roller-coaster. It was over so quickly that Aggie wanted to do it again, but I was green and not agreeable. The boys were putting on quite a show with holding our purses as they sat beside each other on the bench, while we were gone.

Over the forty years we vacationed together, there were many memorable moments, like the fishing trips into Quebec that were unforgettable. I recall playing hop-scotch on the dirt road, only stopping our game long enough to watch a fox cross the road a hundred yards ahead. We were always treated like royalty by our hosts on those wilderness camping trips. They even built us an outdoor outhouse between two trees and hung a roll of toilet paper from the tree too.

Aggies loved her flower gardens and picking wild flowers, like lady slippers, and jack in the pulpits. She even showed me how to fashion a necklace out of daisies. When she and Gord got married in the garden at their home in Oshawa, I picked the biggest bunch of lilacs I could carry and placed them inside and out. Even now when the air becomes heavy in the scent of lilacs I visualize Aggie, so happy and so beautiful that day.

After both of us became widows, we also became travelling companions. We took a few cruises together in the Caribbean and marvelled at the awesome beauty of the ships and the islands we toured. We both felt like princesses. On one of those vacations, Aggie fell in the shower and broke her arm in two places. That night I stayed on a gurney in the hospital quarters beside her. The hospital area was much bigger than our tiny state room and we wondered if this would be considered an upgrade.

On another cruise we took along a bunch of beaded elastic bracelets and called them Bitch Bracelets. The idea supposedly was to give one to anyone in our group who was caught bitching. Aggie made up her own rules and gave them to anyone she heard complaining even if she didn't know them. Soon she became known on board as the bitch lady. Then typical Aggie, decided she liked the bracelets, so she changed her approach and started making up complaints about everything and demanding a bracelet from the rest of us. Soon she had them up both arms. She held the title of the bitchiest even though in reality, she rarely ever complained about anything. She did love to collect things though, like bitch bracelets, scavenger hunt prizes on the islands, blue mountain pottery and racks full of spoons.

I realize how lucky I am to have so many great memories to recall and I hope when I cross over my friend Aggie will be there to welcome me home with a glass of cherry whisky and a story to reminisce.

AN AWESOME ODDITY

As if going back to high school after four decades of being absent wasn't strange enough, I was about to discover the oddity of doing so with my adult son.

Rob had left school before he'd completed the necessary credits to receive a graduation certificate. That documentation was compulsory on all job application forms. Even though he held a full-time job, he realised the need for some insurance in the form of a high school diploma. He had two children to support.

My reason was not as essential to my family's welfare; I simply wanted to learn as much as I could about the writing craft, like where to put the commas, to become a better writer. I told myself that it didn't matter to me, if my name was on a diploma, or not. Honestly though; I doubted if I could do the work necessary to achieve one. Most of what I had learned since I left high school in grade nine, was self-taught. From that informal education, I acquired enough common-sense skills to get by, but not enough to build any confidence in my writing ability.

I worked for my husband's home-based trucking company and took care of the office work. My busy life style made night school the only practical option. I was apprehensive about going back to school and was relieved when my son, Rob said he would like to go with me. One of our employees and a close friend also decided to join us.

We signed up for upgrading course two nights a week. The plan was for my son to come to my house for supper on those evenings and we would go to class together.

On top of doubting if I could do the school work, I became even more concerned that my own son was about to find out how little I really knew.

Rob seemed to be under the misguided impression that I was much smarter than I was, because I had helped him with his homework when he was a boy. Now he was a grown man who was going to go back to school with his mother. What had we gotten ourselves into?

We entered the classroom for the first time and I noticed that Rob went directly to the back of the room to find his seat. Although he never said anything, I kind of suspected that he would rather not advertise the fact that he brought his mother to school with him. That was bound to come out in time, but I'd play along and pretend I didn't know who that friendly, good looking, fellow with the charming smile was. I tried to concentrate on my own composure to keep my nerves calm. Being older than the teacher did take some of those jitters away.

I had been away for so long, I wasn't sure I could grasp the curriculum, but in a short time, the teacher, Mrs. Yorke, had built my confidence to a level where I began to believe I could do this. I tackled the homework assignments with vigor to prove her right. Rob on the other hand left his assignments until the last moment and whined about all the effort it took. It is very hard for a Mom not to help her child no matter how old they are, and I did. Nothing had changed in that department, except, Rob called me, Teachers Pet and Brown Nosier.

His popularity grew nightly, as our class mates gathered around him during break, laughing at his witty sense of humour. Any attempts we originally made to disguise our relationship never lasted for long. All doubt was removed, when I cleaned the smudge of spaghetti sauce from his face with my licked thumb, something only a Mom would do.

By the end of that first term we had both somehow managed a passing grade and willingly signed ourselves up for the compulsory grade 12 English class together. Mrs. Blackstock gallantly introduced us to the confusing works of William Shakespeare and surprisingly we passed. Both of us needed several more credits to reach our goal. Rob took Physical Education and I tackled the Writer's Craft course. While he was doing sit ups and throwing balls through hoops, I was learning how to build plots, handle dialogue and use metaphors to enhance a scene.

Unfortunately; our days of being school mates were soon to end. Rob's hours of work increased, and he had to leave the adult education program. But, I was lucky enough over the next few years to reach my goal.

When graduation night arrived, I walked onto that stage with a confidence that I had not felt before. Every member of my family along with several friends took up two rows of seats in that hot auditorium, to watch me receive my diploma and to hear the valedictory address, I was honoured to present.

Leading a standing ovation, that followed, was my son Rob. The pride on his face was as genuine as the happiness that swept over me. I felt like an eagle taking flight towards a new beginning. The fear and doubts that haunted me when I first returned to school had vanished. I learned that my illusive dreams were obtainable so long as I keep on trying and never gave up on them.

BANKING YOUR ASSETS

      The first indication that unusual calamities were about to plague Fred's day, should have registered when he overslept and woke up to find the bed sheet tangled around his neck. Perhaps that had some bearing on why his memory was playing tricks on him too.

      He could not find his watch, though he swore he had left it on the dresser, nor could he locate the only belt he owned that would fit through the loop holes of the baggy jeans he put on. In a fit of exasperation, he threw the useless belts helter-skelter on the bed, rejecting them all.

      Then his morning coffee, that he hoped would calm his jangled nerves, was upset by his wife's annoying persistence that it was Friday, the day he usually took care of their banking and not Thursday, as he thought. After his know it all wife proved her point on the computer, Fred grabbed the bank deposit book that contained their company deposits of cheques and cash, from her hand and slammed the door on his way out.

His car keys flew out of his hand when he pulled them from the unlocked car door and fell into a mud puddle. That added to his annoyance even more. Provoked by all the aggravation that seemed to be vexing his life, Fred proceeded to wear the battery down and needed a boost to get it to start. He promised to buy himself a new belt and replace the worn-out battery when he was finished at the bank.

Fridays were always busy days at the bank and this one was no exception. Even at this early hour, people were lined up in the roped-off semi-circle, waiting for an available teller. Fred entered through the first set of plate glass doors, but when he opened the second ones, the bankbook slipped out of his hands and its contents of cheques and money flew all over the floor. "Damn it!" he muttered loud enough to bring it to the attention of anyone who hadn't already noticed his clumsiness.

He bent down, picking up the strewn items with both hands, but when he stood back up; his trousers fell to the floor. There he was; the center of attention in his happy face boxer shorts, giving new meaning to the bank's motto, "bank your assets with us." And from the soundless restrain that filled the bank, Fred could tell before he looked, everyone there was suspended in a hypnotic state of shock, With a sheepish grin on his face, he transferred the documents to one hand, awkwardly pulling his pants up with the other and announced, "I knew this was going to happen; it's just been one of those days!"

An explosion of laughter followed his feeble explanation, but he could tell this was one of those embarrassing situations that score the highest level of humour when it happens to someone else. The surveillance camera even captured his performance, and the tellers at the Scotia bank had a hard time serving him with a straight face, from that day on.

BARBARA ANN SCOTT

Marilyn Andrews was a black girl whose family lived next door to the house my parents rented, on the east side of Toronto. We were the same age and spent our pre-school years together, playing with our dolls. None of the century old houses on our street in East York, had driveways but some of them had a front veranda, as did the one I lived in. That small outdoor space magically became a play house for Marilyn and me.

I don't recall ever being invited inside Marilyn's home, nor do I remember her being in mine. The only thread of racial discrimination that entered into our young lives though, was the fact that she had no white dolls and I had no coloured ones. We both thought that was odd. She adored my Barbara Ann Scott doll, and dreamed of becoming a figure skater herself, one day, and I loved playing with her Topsy baby with its side glancing eyes and comical grin. I intended to ask Santa to bring me one for Christmas, but before winter arrived, both Marilyn and I became very ill.

When my mother found out that Marilyn was diagnosed with Polio, she was terrified that I had contacted it too. Thankfully, I was spared that misery, but my little friend was not as lucky. She spent months in the hospital recovering but was left crippled by the disease. I felt so sorry for her. She had to learn to walk with braces on both of her legs and her dream of figure skating was never to be realised.

When my parents told me we were moving away, I was heartbroken and so was Marilyn. I gave her my Barbara Ann Scott doll to remember me by and she gave me her Topsy baby.

After we moved to Scarborough, I never saw Marilyn again but her Topsy doll survived through two generations of my family and was loved by them all. I wondered if Marilyn had kept my Barbara Ann Scott doll too. Over the years, I looked in second hand stores and antique shops for a replacement of the skating legion doll, but to no avail. The only one I located was displayed in a museum and not for sale.

Those dolls are over 60 years old and were modeled after a very special Canadian. From 1940 to 1948, she was known as Canada's sweetheart in the world of figure skating. Barbara Ann Scott had won the junior title in 1940 and continued her rise to fame by winning the Canadian Woman's Championship, followed by the American Championship, and The European Worlds. In 1948, she took the Olympic gold medal in St. Mortz, Switzerland. That accomplishment was achieved on a slushy outdoor rink that was full of ruts from hockey being played on the ice before her performance.

With her Olympic gold medal around her neck, she was welcomed home by large crowds of exuberant fans. Parades were held in her honour and the market was soon flooded with Barbara Ann Scott dolls. Every little girl, including me wanted one of them dressed in a skating costume and wearing ice skates on her feet.

After her retirement from amateur sports, Barbara went pro and replaced Sonja Henie as the star performer in the show, Hollywood on Ice. She was inducted into the Canadian Sports Hall Of Fame in 1955.

I was telling my neighbour Mary that I found a Barbra Ann Scott doll in a museum just like the one I used to have and she told me she still had hers. I begged to see it. It was identical to mine, pink skating costume and all. I told her if she ever wanted to sell it to let me know and she did. You can imagine the joy I felt when Mary accepted my offer of $50, for the doll.

    I took her to the Antique Road Show but they said without the original box, she had no collector value. Maybe not to them, but she sure does to me. I really wish I could share this memory with Marilyn. I wonder if she still has her Barbara Ann Scott doll too.

BAREFOOT MEMORY

In the semi-conscious state that lies between deep slumber and being fully awake, Laurie restlessly tossed in her bed, disturbed by what she thought were mice gnawing at the bedroom walls, of the century old homestead they called home. She pulled the corner of her pillow over her exposed ear to stifle the noise.

Into her hazy sleep shrouded mind, crept the pungent odour of burnt toast, agitating her more. She tugged at her pillow, turning her face into it, hoping the illusion would vanish and sleep would return, but the pillow also held the stench of burnt toast.

"Damn it," she attempted to utter, but what escaped her lips was a raspy hoarse whisper, queerly undetectable as her own voice. Her throat felt dry and parched like sandpaper. An unpleasant taste seemed to overpower her senses. She swallowed, but to no avail, as there seemed to be no moisture left in her mouth.

It's no use! I'll never get back to sleep now, she thought, remembering how long it had taken her to accomplish that task earlier in the evening, while her mind kept anguishing over her first day of high school, scheduled to begin in the morning.

More than anything else, she wanted to fit in. That single aspiration had led Laurie down a materialistic path where her top priorities centred on brand named clothing and shoes, expensive items her family refused to buy. She saved the money she made babysitting all summer and bought herself a pair of designer jeans and brand name sports shoes, in hopes that they would ensure her acceptance to the, 'in crowd'.

Her parents were far too old-fashioned and prudent to shop for their four children anywhere except discount stores. Sometimes Laurie wished she was an only child, because everything she owned was either passed down from her older sister Karen or came with a clearance tag attached. Everything except the brand named running shoes and expensive jeans that were folded neatly on the chair in her room. Those she had bought at a boutique store in the mall with her own money.

Besides the rest of her bargain basement wardrobe, she was also embarrassed by the shabby old farm house they lived in and did not like sharing a bedroom with her bossy older sister, Karen. But what she hated even more were those pesky field mice that were making an awful racket inside her wall. It sounded like they were cracking nuts and hissing at one another. She hit the wall with her fist, but the noise continued.

Reluctantly she reached for the lamp on the bedside table between the two beds and switched it on. The room was full of a murky, billowing, grey fog that was rolling up the slope of the ceiling, completely obscuring the window at the opposite end of the room. Like a hot searing poker, the horror was branded into her brain, sending shock waves throughout her body.

    Laurie threw back the covers and bolted from her bed, coughing and choking. Uncontrollable fear made her breathing become laboured and rapid, while her heart thundered in her chest. Stumbling she fell upon her sister's bed, violently shaking her, but with no response.
.

    "Fire! Karen, wake up! The house is on fire!" Still there was no response. "Oh God, she can't be dead," she cried, pushing her sister's body out of the bed and onto the floor.

    "What?" Karen retorted, after being so rudely awakened.

    "The house is on fire! Get up! We must wake the Others," Laurie croaked, holding her throat.

"Oh my God!" Karen cackled, realizing this was real and not just a bad dream. "You go to Robbie's room and I'll get Bonnie," she said taking charge as usual.

Together they groped their way through the smoke engulfed hall towards the separate bedrooms of their younger sister and brother. Their cheeks were stained with tears from the eye stinging smoke and the nightmare fear that gripped their hearts.

When Karen discovered her little sister's cot was empty, panic robbed her of any sense of reasoning she had left. "Where is Bonnie?" she groaned, dropping to her knees and crawling around on the floor. She thought the tot may have fallen out of bed or be hiding under the bed or in the closet. Tears of torment streamed from her eyes as she struggled to find her.

"Maybe she's downstairs with Mom and Dad," Robbie cawed from the doorway, rubbing his burning eyes with his pyjama sleeves. His friend who had stayed overnight was standing beside him, just as frightened.

"I can't breathe!" Laurie affirmed. "If we don't get out of here now, we're all going to die," she added, pulling her younger brother towards the stair case.

Karen frantically continued to search the closets and the floor on her hands and knees, refusing to go downstairs with the others, knowing if Bonnie was up there, she couldn't survive much longer, but neither could she.

Laurie, Robbie and his friend Johnny, stumbled down the murky stairway and ran into their parents' bedroom. Out of breath, hacking and choking, they switched on the light, and before even announcing to her parents that the house was on fire, Laurie shouted as loud as she could, in her hoarse voice, "Bonnie is safe! She's with Mom and Dad."

Karen could barely understand what Laurie said. Her voice sounded like a record being played at slow speed. The smoke inhalation was affecting her brain. Disorientated and beginning to feel faint, her body refused to crawl any further and became consumed in a violent coughing fit. Seconds later she felt her father's strong arms lifting her up, but it was not until she reached the cool night air, that she fully regained her senses.

Huddled together they heard the sirens of the approaching fire trucks. They gazed in horror upon the flames leaping through the girl's upstairs bedroom window, destroying their belongings, but the brand-named shoes and designer jeans were no longer of any importance. Every member of the family was keenly aware of how lucky they were to have escaped the inferno. From that moment on, they vowed to always cherish the memory of the night when their most valued possessions stood together, barefoot on the cold wet grass.

BEFORE TELEVISION

I was born before television became a household necessity. Back during the 1940s, entertainment was self-made. Families and neighbours gathered on their front porches during the mild months and played musical instruments together. They sang and laughed and swapped funny jokes and stories. Listening to a lively tune or a talented storyteller was always a pleasurable way to share leisure time.

The radio filled the air waves with all kinds of programming besides music. Some of my favorite radio shows were, The Nelson Family, and Red Skelton, but the Alfred Hitchcock Hour and the Inner-sanctum with its creaky door sound, both scared the begeepers out of me. Before television, people went to movie theaters or took in plays and concerts for entertainment.

People were more social back then. Families and friends shared their daily experiences and happy times with each other. Long distance relationships were continued through writing letters and stamps cost two pennies each. There was a time before T.V., when most people never had a telephone, unless they were rich. And those who did were probably on a shared party line with several other households. A crank handle on the side of the wooden phone allowed you to make different rings to reach someone on your line. Ours was two longs and a short. Telephone operators had to place long distance calls for you, through their switch board. Nosey parkers could easily listen in to another party's conversation by simply lifting the receiver to their ear. Private networking between family and friends was best accomplished with pen and paper.

      Before we had our first T.V., I knew the last names of everyone that lived on my short street, in Scarborough. They were always addressed as Mr. and Mrs., and never by a first name. We played on the street, ran through their yards, played hop-scotch on their side walks and dropped our bikes on their lawns. I don't recall ever being scolded for running around on a neighbour's property. Most of the dogs in the neighbourhood ran around with us and we knew them all by name too. There was no sitting in front of a television set for hours on end. We were told to go out and play and we did.

Our play consisted of outdoor activities and self-run sports games that were unsupervised by coaches or parents. We walked to school by ourselves too. We fought our own battles and never needed psychologists to decide how we should deal with the bullies in life. No one progressed to the next grade level unless they completed the work with a passing grade. And if you misbehaved at school, you got the strap at home and at school.

Being called names was no reason to go crying to your parents. We were taught to say this rhyme. "Sticks and stones will break my bones, but names will never hurt me." Before T.V. kids rode bicycles without helmets, swam in polluted creeks, drank water out of the garden hose and slurped on ice chips sheared off the Lake Simcoe Ice truck at his delivery stops We ate berries off the bush without washing them first and built forts that could have caved in on us or caught the field and ourselves on fire, from the candles we lit, and we lived.

In my home I was twelve years old when we got our first television. I remember it well. It was an Admiral T.V., set into a big box, but the screen was very small, 10 inches, I think. There programing was only on during the day. We used a set of rabbit ears for an antenna. By turning the rabbit ears around, if we were lucky we could pick up a couple of local fuzzy stations. Those we also lost when the weather was bad. Then the screen would turn so snowy we would strain our eyes trying to make out the picture and it was impossible to see the puck during the hockey game.

      Sometimes a tube in the back of the boxy T.V. would stop working and before a television repair man was called, my father would try to fix it himself. It was difficult for him to be sure which tube it was that had to be replaced, so he would remove several of them and trot off to the corner store where a tube testing machine was making the proprietor rich. After the culprit had been identified and replaced, it was not uncommon for our television set to still refuse to work. Then and only then would a television repair man be called in to fix the problem. There were buttons to lighten the screen and others to stop it from rolling. Regardless of the frustration television brought into our lives it also brought us much knowledge and pleasurable entertainment. Our world instantly became a much smaller place, thanks to the men and women who gave us our first glimpse of far off lands, through the lens of their television cameras.

Life before television was perhaps more nostalgic, but I am happy to sit in my lazy boy chair and watch my favorite programing. I wouldn't want to go back to the times before T.V, that's for sure. Would you?

BIPPITY BOOPITY BOO

A baby girl was welcomed into this world on Sept 25, 1990 with more fan-fair than what usually would accompany the tenth grandchild born into a family. She was named, Heather after her young aunt who had lost her life in a car accident, twenty years before this child's birth. When her parents, Bonnie and Brian Sheppard, announced their new baby girl would be named Heather, all of us felt a tug on our heart strings. Grandparents, Aunts and Uncles lined up to see this child who was named after an angel. She was beautiful. No princess could have been more adored.

Heather was not destined to live the life of a princess though. Her unique individuality caused her to be teased and bullied throughout her younger school years. Eventually her kind heart and radiant smile became her saving grace. It was meeting Adam, her prince charming, that gave her the confidence to follow her heart. They met and fell in love when she was still in school and working part time at a deli. He worked there too along with her mother, Bonnie. Heather was a vegetarian and working in a deli wasn't what she wanted to do, for rest of her life.

School was not easy for Heather, but she always put forth her best effort. Adam encouraged her to go on and not give up. She did take a course in giving manicures and pedicures, but even though it satisfied her artsy talent, it did nothing to build her moral. She was not happy, but soon that changed, when she signed up for a nursing course. She was delighted to receive her Personal Support Worker degree and enjoyed the satisfying work of helping others with their home care.

When she and Adam fell in love, so young, I worried that it wouldn't last, or they might move too fast, but that was not the case. They patiently waited until she finished her training before they set their marriage date. It was destined to be a celebration of their love that had grown over five years of courtship. They had some money saved but not enough to pay for all the wedding festivities, when the manicure company Heather worked for at that time, went out of business; causing unforeseen financial hardship. Money was in short supply so the expenses had to be kept as low as possible.

To keep the cost down, a Friday night wedding was arranged. The hall was an old court house in Newcastle with a gazebo outside where the service was to take place followed by the reception inside the quaint old, castle like, architectural building. The bridal party's flowers, the photography, the wedding cake and the centerpieces had been designed by the talented hands of themselves, their family and friends and the photography were looked after by her cousin, Shannon.

On the day of my granddaughter's wedding, the tables and chairs along with the boxes full of wine glasses were stacked along the wall when my daughters, Karen and Laurie and I arrived the morning of the wedding to, awaiting the arrival of some members of the family to help set the hall up.

Heather was coming to help too but my daughter Karen and I were the first to arrive. When I entered the hall, my attention was drawn to four beautiful sheer swags with fairy lights inside, draped from the chandelier in the centre of the hall to the side walls. "How beautiful, "I exclaimed in awe, only to be told there had been a mistake. The rental company was on its way to remove the swags. They were not supposed to be installed until the following day for the Sat wedding party.

When the rental company arrived, I had a conversation with the man who came to remove the lighted swags and asked how much they would charge to leave them in place for my granddaughters wedding. He informed me there was also a sheer, lighted backdrop for behind the head table that he had on the truck to install for the wedding tomorrow. He called his boss and the price they quoted to rent both the items was within my grasp and less than a quarter of the regular amount for the rental of such fine, elegant decor.

I gladly paid him the money and waited in excited anticipation for Heather to arrive. As I watched the room becoming transformed into a fairy book wedding chapel, I couldn't help but wonder if her Aunt Heather in heaven wasn't orchestrating these unplanned events for her name sake.

When Heather arrived, I hurried to her car. "I have a wedding gift for you in the hall," I informed her.

"Grandma, you have already given me enough," she stated, meaning the money I had put in the card envelope and given in advance to help with the expense.

I walked by her side as she entered the hall. The look of awe on her face and the tears of joy in her eyes when she saw how stunningly beautiful everything looked, was priceless. I felt like the fairy god mother who waved her wand and uttered the words "Bippidy, boppidy, boo", and presto the castle was ready for our beautiful Cinderella and her handsome prince.

The wedding was fit for a princess and I hope they will always be as in love as they were on their wedding day. It was by far one of the happiest days of my life too. Playing a fairy godmother doesn't happen in real life very often. I am grateful I got to experience the pleasure on Heathers's wedding day.

BOATING ACCIDENT RESCUE

John and his brother Len raced the 45 horse power outboard engine as fast as it would go to propel the boat through the rough waters on Jacks Lake. They were heading straight towards the over turned row boat, in hopes of finding Len's two Grandsons, Dillon and Charlie afloat, nearby. The boys had been told at least once every day since they arrived at the lake a month ago, that they were not allowed to take the row boat out unless they were wearing life jackets. Those jackets were lying on the dock where the nine and ten-year-old boys had left them. Len had tossed them into the motor boat when he left on this rescue mission.

Jane paced frantically on the dock praying the swimming lessons she had insisted the boys take last winter would save her sons from drowning. The waves on the lake were so high with the storm moving in that even an Olympic swimmer would have difficulty staying afloat. She wanted to go with her Dad and Uncle but realised they were right; she needed to stay on shore in case something went wrong with their motor boat. She could call for help.

John detested the smart aleck kids and the way they talked back to their mother and grandfather. They were his nephews, so he tolerated them, but he was secretly hoping this episode would be enough to send Jane and the little brats packing. *I don't wish them dead though*, he thought as he steered his craft closer to the overturned row boat.

Len took off his life jacket and leapt into the water before the boat was stopped. He could not see either of his grandson's anywhere nearby. He dove under the overturned craft and there they were in the pocket of air left below the bow. Both were crying in fright. They clung to the floatation cushion that had been on the seat. Len gave a sigh of relief and ignored the pain in his chest and arm.

"Take a big breath, and I will get you out of here one at a time," he told them as he reached for the youngest one first. Down into the dark water he dove with his grandson in his arms. When he surfaced his face was red, a sure sign his blood pressure was soaring. John reached over the side of the rocking boat and pulled Charlie into it and Len disappeared under the water again. It took a long time for him to come back up. John was just about to go overboard after his seventy-eight-year old brother when they surfaced, on the opposite side of the overturned boat.

"Hang on, I'm coming," John called out over a loud boom of thunder and a flash of fork lightening that hit somewhere very close by. *Damn these kids* he thought as he struggled to maneuver the boat to where Len and his nephew were splashing about, struggling to stay afloat. The rain now pelted down on them.

"Throw us the life jackets to hold onto," Len called out, He had removed his to dive for the boys.

John did as he asked, but only one landed within easy reach, He brought the boat to rest beside them and reached over to help bring the youngster in.

Dillon was hauled to safety, but Len was suffering too much chest pain to climb over the side of the boat. John gave his brother his own life jacket and a rope to hold onto, before he started towing him through the rough water, back to shore.

"If I ever hear tell of you two getting into a boat without wearing a life jacket, I will hunt you down and kick your ass," he sternly warned. For once they never made a smart aleck reply.

"What about the row boat, Uncle John, "Dillon asked.

"It will probably drift to shore. We will look for it tomorrow. There won't be any more row boat for you two to fish in, that's for sure, "he gruffly replied, letting them know those privileges were taken away for the rest of this summer. "Be more concerned about your grandfather than the damn boat," he added.

Their rocking craft made it to the shore intact. Jane could see the stress her father was in, when John helped her lift him out of the water and onto the dock. She knew he was having a heart attack and felt awful that her boys were what caused it. He needed medical attention immediately. She ran up to the cottage, started her car and backed it down the hill to the dock where Len was placed in the back seat and covered with a blanket. He was shaking miserably. Jane rushed him to the nearest hospital in Bancroft, as fast as she could, leaving John behind to deal with his nephews.

Just what I didn't need, John thought.

The boys were afraid of their gruff uncle. He was mean to them from the time they were little. He was nothing like their grandfather, who they had wrapped around their baby fingers

"I sure hope Grandpa will be alright," Charlie said when they entered the cottage.

"Me too," Dillon agreed.

There was no reply from John. He knew his brother had been getting angina for quite some time and refused to go to the doctor. He thought he should say something to reassure the kids that their grandfather would survive, but he didn't think he would. Len looked like death warmed over when they left.

John was right. His brother died before they reached the hospital and although they tried to revive him his worn-out heart refused to restart. Jane drove back to the cottage with tears on her face and an ache in her heart. Her Dad was her hero. He helped her get back on her feet after her messy divorce from the boys cheating father and paid her rent when the deadbeat never made his child support payments. Her father on the other hand, was such a great Dad and she would miss him terribly.

She also wondered what her Uncle John would do now. Both of their wives had died young and the two brothers had lived together at the cottage since there retirements fifteen years ago. John had no children. He said he never wanted any, but Jane felt he was putting on an act and he really did like her boys, even if he wouldn't show it. She thought she might stay on with her Uncle for the rest of the summer, but she would ask him first. He was a funny old duck.

Johns answer was a loud and clear "No."

Jane packed up their things and headed back to the city to make the funeral arrangements. John promised he would come along and stay until the service was over.

The boys remained quiet and withdrawn through it all. It was so unlike them. They were suffering from guilt syndrome and felt it was their fault that their grandfather died by having a heart attack while trying to save them.

John recognized the problem and put down his gruff uncle act. He hugged the boys and said, "I'm sorry for the mean way I treated you. It wasn't your fault that grandpa died. I wanted to jump into the lake and try to save you, but he insisted he wanted to do it. He could be mighty stubborn. I also want you to know he was having heart problems before you came to the cottage and he wouldn't go to the doctor, the old fool. So, don't go blaming yourself for what happened," he told them.

The boys both hugged him back.

"You're the best uncle," Dillon said.

John laughed. "Yah, I'm the only one you got too."

"I promise we will be better when we come to the cottage next time and we won't do anything wrong like go in a boat without a life jacket on,"

"I can't wait," John said a little sarcastically. After all he did have an image to up-hold.

BOOM TOWN FORT MCMURRAY

Many adventurous souls have been lured by the promise of making big money to the Athabasca Oil Sands, in northern Alberta. Big oil conglomerates have invested huge amounts of money into this massive project. The incentive to entice people to live and work so far north is higher wages than they could possibly make elsewhere. The average yearly income in Fort McMurray Alberta was $189,000, in 2013.

The excavation of the oil is done by water fracking. The contaminated water used to strip the sand of its oil, is then stored in tailing ponds and the stripped sand lays piled in dunes where once the forest thrived. Massive acres of land in the middle of the boreal forest lay in barren waste, making the landscape look like the surface of the moon. But, I was happy to see that the oil companies responsible for the destruction of the natural terrain, were reforesting the land once the extraction was completed. They also installed noise boomers that keep birds and animals away from the polluted tailing ponds. That same water is reused in the oil extraction method to reduce the amount of contamination.

The machinery and heavy equipment used in the process looks like giant prehistoric monsters. The conveyer fed buildings where the crude oil is collected and piped to the refineries all over Canada and the USA, also looked strange and monstrous to me. The scope of this process is so enormous it can be seen from outer space.

My daughter Bonnie and son-in-law Brian joined the ever increasing migration to Fort McMurray, also known as Fort McMoney, several years ago. In August, 2015, I visited them and was surprised at what I discovered.

The town is nestled in the middle of the Boreal forest in a valley where 3 rivers converge on their route north to the Arctic Ocean. According to an information pamphlet I acquired, the population in Fort McMurray has grown by 125% since the year 2000. Between permanent residents and the temporary on sight workers, there is approximately the same amount of people living there as in Oshawa, my home town.

The average age of the population is between 25 and 29. There is plenty of entertainment and recreational facilities to satisfy that age bracket. Many young families are calling Fort McMurray their permanent home, but there are not many grey haired seniors visible. There certainly are many diverse nationalities. People come from all over the world, but a high percentages are from eastern Canada making it a friendly place to live and visit.

There is construction everywhere. Wide expansive highways and bridges spanning the Athabasca, Snye and Clearwater rivers that flow through the town are impressive. Although there are new subdivisions cropping up throughout the hills that surround the area, the majority of people are still apartment dwellers or live on sight. Eighty thousand on-site living accommodations are available in long rows of barracks at the oil sands, an hour's drive north of Fort McMurray.

The cost of housing is ridiculously high. The 2 bedroom apartment my daughter rents is considered cheap at $2000 a month. The cost to buy a used trailer in a trailer park ranged from 250 to 400 thousand and new homes can top a million.

Fort McMurray has short warm summers and long cold winters. When I visited in Aug it was near 30 most days but dipped to the low teens at night. I found it strange that there were very few flower pots on balconies of the apartment complexes and no gardens or pools in the yards of the homes. Perhaps because of the shortness of the growing season or perhaps many folks are only there temporarily. As for winter, it averages minus 18 but has dipped as low as minus 57. Snow falls over a seven month span from Oct to April and averages around 134 cm per season. Because of the severe cold, salt does not work on the roads, sand is used instead. It makes for a dusty dirty scenario when winter ends and the massive cleanup begins. Everything is covered in dust and sand from the winter road maintenance.

I found the prices in grocery stores were slightly higher, but all the service was much more expensive. I had lunch at the senior centre with a friend one day. The daily special was, three times higher than at the Oshawa Senior Citizen's Center. I went swimming at the luxury recreational facility that Suncor oil and the City of Fort McMurray built. It was also three times more than where I swim in Oshawa. Haircuts were even more extravagantly priced in comparison. Large box stores and food chains were established in the malls around town making it convenient to shop. Everything has to be trucked in year round adding to the cost of all items.

    The closest major city is Edmonton; 439 km south. There is only one highway between them. In The Wood Buffalo district, where Fort McMurray is located, there are some very remote communities that can only be reached in the winter on Ice roads across frozen water.

    As my daughter was driving me back to the brand new international airport, on the outskirts of town we passed a sign on the highway which read, Next gas station 200 km. I guess all those folks driving pickup trucks and SUVs wouldn't want to leave Fort Mac without a full tank.

    I am glad I made the trip. It was much different than I expected. It is a boom town under construction. It was friendly and full of job opportunity. I may have bit the bullet too in my younger years, but I'm retired now and perfectly content to call Oshawa, Ontario my home.

    Since I wrote this article, a wild fire had ravished the area, destroying many of those million-dollar new homes built on the hills surrounding the town. It has become the biggest forest fire in Canadian history and also the most expensive. I predict we will all see a rise in our insurance rates because of it. Fort McMurray will be re-established and hopefully with more safety and thought given to fire prevention, but many of its former residents, like my daughter will not go back.

BUCKET LIST

    My bucket list has changed many times over the years. Some things did get accomplished and crossed off, like graduating from high school at 50 years of age, and buying a home in the country. Others got revised or condensed from their original anticipation. An example of that would be my wish to have twelve children. It became less than half that amount once maturity and reality entered my senses. Other items were simply erased because I lost interest in them or realised, I did not have the talent necessary to become a famous movie star, singer or figure skater.

    The bucket list I'd write at this stage of my life would still include a few of the things I have always coveted, like becoming a published author and travelling to see more of the world while I'm still able to do so and enjoy it. Having enough money to be able to afford to travel the world would be nice too.

    Winning a big lottery is no longer important to me though, because I do not believe that any amount of money could alter the happiness in my life. Happiness is a state of mind and has nothing to do with being rich. It would be fun to share the winnings with others though; so I wouldn't turn it down, if I ever was that lucky.

Finding the time to publish the 200 poems my mother wrote during her life time is something I want to do starting now. Sending my children's stories out to more publishers is also doable. Writing the memoirs of all the adventures I have encountered on my personal journey is a future endeavour on my bucket list, along with spending more time with the children in my family. They inspire me and put a fresh perspective on living in the moment.

I think I would like to give more of myself to others. I miss volunteering at the food bank. I may go back there a day a week and maybe do some reading in the nursing homes for those whose eyes are no longer able to see. I would also like to hear their life stories.

I would like to find a church where I belong or feel comfortable in. It will likely be the Salvation Army, as it was the church of choice for my parents too. I never thought I would become a member there, but the older I get, the more I find their philosophy and their charity close to my heart.

    Whether or not I accomplish these things on my bucket list doesn't matter all that much because I have enjoyed the ride so far and am grateful for all the gifts I am still receiving. What will be, will be.

CANADA DAY AT LAKEVIEW PARK

If you want to see Canadian pride at its finest, come to Lakeview Park, in Oshawa, on Canada Day. The park is situated on the beautiful shores of Lake Ontario and is the location of celebration for the patriotic folks who live in the motor city.

I like to arrive early in the afternoon, before it becomes too crowded to stake out a spot for my lawn chair, under one of the big shade trees that line the walk way along the shore of the lake. Some folks like to sit facing the water, but I prefer to place myself, facing towards the pathway, allowing me the best view of Canada's proudest as they stroll on by.

Red and white are the colours of the day. Red maple leafs appear on all sorts of tee shirts, hats and stick pins. Some even have them painted on their cheeks and tattooed on their arms. The Canadian flag also shows up on many garments, tote bags and lawn chairs. There are some amid the crowd, who wear our flag around their shoulders like a cape, and proudly strut their stuff, Bat Man style.

Others, it seems, have the occasion mixed up with Halloween and think that wearing a red and white umbrella hat and goofy sun glasses is patriotic. To those Canadian clowns it probably is. Then there are the rednecks, looking like they are going to a hillbilly hoe down in their tattered cut offs and the cowboys in their Stetson hats. Add to that, some girls in long skirts and peasant blouses while others get the boys attention while wearing short shorts and tiny halter tops. Toss in a handful of very large folks who haven't been told that Spandex will only stretch so far. But, regardless of their size, or how they are dressed, every one of them came to the Canada day celebrations for the same reason, to display their pride in our country.

The little children run about chasing seagulls and waving flags. They are happy to dance to the music being played on the make shift stage, or romp about the playground, toss stones into the lake or climb upon the rocks along the waters edge. There are lots of venders in the park to entice their parents to buy them food, treats or pop. There is an amusement park area where the children's games and the entertainment are free and a firs aid post.

Most teenagers saunter about in groups with overly giddy friends. The girls dressed in their too tight pants and the boys in their too loose ones. Each has a cell phone in their grasp. Some carry on conversations with absent friends while dodging around everyone else on the path.

Then there are the young lovers, so easy to spot amongst the growing throngs of people. Arm in arm they move as one, in and out of the tightening pack. They look at each other with such longing, as if they're possessed with passion. Some are and need to be reminded that it's not considered very polite or patriotic to make out on a blanket, amongst a crowd of Canada Day patriots.

Young parents pushing strollers and pulling wagons find an empty spot on the bank to spread their blanket down. The shuttle buses continue to bring people to the event and the groups along the grassy bank, begin to tighten up as twilight arrives. More and more people attempt to share the limited space along the shore, in order to have a front row seat for the amazing fireworks display. .

Although I enjoy watching the fireworks explode in glorious cascades of colour above the calm waters of Lake Ontario, I think what I enjoy even more is watching the parade of people who gather at Lakeview Park on Canada Day.

CASEY

Before Casey became my daughter's dog, she belonged to friends who had rescued her from an animal shelter in Texas. She had been treated there for life threatening injuries suffered at the hands of a cruel and despicable man. She had a belly full of surgical scars and a deeply rooted fear of men wearing work boots, to prove it.

Her humane rescuers fell in love with the gentle animal, adopted her and brought her with them when they moved back to Canada. But Casey never traveled well. She was car sick and frightened, the whole way from Dallas Texas to Oshawa, Ontario. Consequently; when another career move back down south was eminent, they decided not to put the dog through that trauma again and kindly, gave her to my daughter Bonnie and her family.

Casey resembled a miniature shepherd and looked a little bit like Scoobydo. We learned that her breed was used to round up cattle in Texas, and that explained why she loved to run. Her destiny was to become a dear companion to every member of our family, over her long-life time.

    The first time I met Casey, I tripped and fell in the door towards her, frightening her so badly she peed right there, on the floor. I felt so bad about scaring her. She soon forgave my clumsiness, though.

    During the years Bonnie and her family lived in the apartment at my house, Casey and I became walking buddies. Before long, she knew the route to the park so well that if one of the kids left the gate open, she would take herself for a walk there. After a good run about, if no one showed up with her leash, she would walk herself home again too.

    I missed her when my daughter and her family moved away. But after their town house caught fire from faulty wiring to the dryer, they were forced to stay at the Holiday Inn until the renovations were made. I immediately offered to keep Casey until they were able to return to their home. The dog had no way of knowing what our intentions were, but she let me know that she didn't want to go back to the burned-out town house. She hid behind me, whimpering, while the others were getting ready to leave for their first night at the Holiday Inn. I reassured her that she was safe with me and she seemed to understand.

Dogs were not allowed on their floor, at the hotel, but every weekend they smuggled Casey into the elevator and into their quarters for a short visit. Even the house cleaning staff turned a blind eye to the unregistered guest. They knew that these three children were homeless and the love from their little dog who was always overjoyed to see them, brought hope that life would return to normal soon. During the rest of the time she and I were inseparable as we walked throughout the neighbourhood. She was well behaved around other dogs and women or children but backed away if a strange man tried to pat her. That fear would never go away.

Shortly after my daughter and her family moved back into the townhouse, they sold it and bought a house around the corner from me, I was delighted, because Casey and I could continue the walking exercise that benefited us both. From then on, if Casey escaped from her yard she would visit the park, and me, in that order. She knew exactly where she was going.

As the years slipped by, our walks became slower and we covered shorter distances. Some days neither of us felt like it, but we went for the sake of our friend on the other end of the leash. Time was taking its toll on Casey. Her muzzle turned grey, her cataract eyes could no longer see the squirrels she loved to chase, and she became deaf. Other problems that go along with old age also plagued her, like seizures that left her jaw chattering and a bladder that was unable to hold urine until someone got home to let her out. She was humiliated when those accidents occurred. She also needed assistance to get into the car and could barely climb the stairs into the house.

It was with a sad and heavy heart that Bonnie found the mercy to spare our beloved old friend anymore suffering. She asked me to come with her to the animal clinic that sad day. Before we left, I took my good old pal on one last walk around the block and I let her sniff every hydrant and post along the way for as long as she wanted.

Bonnie and I stayed by her side at the clinic while she took her final breaths. Tears spilled down our cheeks as we patted her head and said goodbye for the last time. Hugging each other for support, we agreed, Casey's gentle and unconditional love will always be remembered by all who received it. She was a good girl and a loyal friend.

CONTINENTAL TURBANS AT THE EX

    During the mid-1950's there was one annual event that caused great anticipation for the kids in the Toronto area. It was the opening of the Canadian National Exhibition in August. The Ex was the highlight of the summer for my friend Gail and I. Dressed in shorts, halter tops and sandals; we climbed aboard the crowded bus and streetcar. Our life savings of eight dollars and the entrance pass the school gave us were tucked in our pockets. This was destined to be a magical day, we thought.

    After we got through the entrance turnstiles we took off on the run to buy a strip of tickets for the mid-way rides. That wicket was lined up a long way back. Slowly the line moved past a vender's stall that sold colourful hats. A couple of exotic, Continental turbans with hair pieces attached attracted our attention. They were only a few dollars and we were rich enough to buy them. Mine was green silk with stiff, red hair that swooped over my forehead. Gail was a red head too, but her turban was blue silk. We both felt so glamorous wearing them.

The ride tickets cost a lot more than we thought they would. With barely enough left for lunch and bus fare home, we headed for the Arial gondola ride that would take us to the far end of the mid-way. Perched high above the sea of people, we could see most of the fair grounds.

"Look, there's the laugh in the dark, "I said while watching a couple of kids come tumbling out of the barrel.

"Yes! And there's the tilt a whirl and the octopus! We'll ride them too," Gail vowed.

We pointed out other attractions as we sailed along above the crowds, wearing our exquisite wigs and turbans. When the aerial ride ended, we headed straight for the roller coaster.

Waiting to board the old wooden structure was half the fun. The excitement kept building with every scream the passengers ahead of us made as they careened their way through the snaky hills and curves. Finally, it was our turn to get on. We sat in the very first car and the safety bars locked us securely in. The fellow who checked the lock told us to take off our hats or we would lose them. I did but there was nowhere to put it, so I stuffed it down the front of my halter top. Now I looked a sight with a red hairy chest sticking out of my halter top.

  The train began to climb higher and higher, until we reached the peak. It seemed to be suspended there for a few seconds before gravity riveted us against the safety bar and lifted us off the seat. Screaming at the top of our lungs, and holding on for dear life, we turned a corner going so fast, I thought the cars would tip over and fall off the track. Again, and again we left our stomachs behind as the coaster thrillingly ran its entire course and came to an abrupt stop. Completely out of breath and barely able to stand, the first words out of my mouth was, "Let's do it again!"

  By noon we had used up all our tickets and we realized if we wanted to spend more time on the midway, we needed more money. That's when we found the Crown and Anchor game and decided to try our luck at doubling our dwindling finances. The plan failed pitifully and now we had no money left to buy lunch, nor to get home. We wandered about aimlessly for a while.

Envious of those who walked by carrying stuffed animals and canes with grinning dolls and monkeys attached, we trudged on, pretending not to notice. Past the bingo tent and all the Carnies who sang out their invitations to play their game and win a prize. There would be no prize for me and Gail to display at home.

The aroma of hot dogs and fried onions floated past us as did kids eating candy floss and taffy apples. Our spirits were low but were lifted when we entered the Purer Food Building and discovered all the free food samples we could get by simply lining up. We came out of there in the late afternoon with full bellies and 2 bags each crammed with pamphlets, paper hats and promotional gifts. Life was good! And keeping that thought in our heads, we were ready to call it a day and walk the five miles home.

We wore our turbans all the way, and even though our feet were complaining, we felt like the queens from Sheba or Siam, or wherever ladies dressed in such exotic fashion came from. The circus would have been a closer guess, I'm sure.

DECORATING DISASTERS OF THE 70's

August 27, 1975. Horrified, we huddled together in those predawn hours, watching flames leap through the walls and lick up the roof of our century old home. Although most of our belongings were being destroyed by the electrically fused fire, I was grateful that my most valued possessions; my husband Fred and our four children were standing beside me, barefoot on the cold wet grass. Everything else could be replaced or rebuilt.

Because of the age of the house and the upgrades needed to pass today's building codes, we took the cash settlement from our insurance company and began the work ourselves. While living in a mobile home on our front lawn we tackled the dirty job of demolition and began our education in rough carpentry. Together with the help of a hired carpenter, along with our family and friends, we worked diligently for four months to be able to move back in before the first major snow fell. In December. We met our goal but, much work still needed to be done including decorating all the rooms.

Interior decorating was my forte. I liked to think I was fairly, creative in the process but, I was not happy with our drywall efforts. We sanded until our arms throbbed and felt like they would fall off, yet the joints were still noticeable even under a coat of sealer. We learned that installing drywall was an art on its own and neither Fred nor I had the expertise for it. Still; rough joints and all, I was delighted to have seven blank rooms waiting for me to decorate. Fred gave me full reign in that department. He painted the ceilings and I happily did the rest.

I was a fan of the popular decorating shows on television and watched in amazement as they transformed plain rooms into ones with elegant ambiance. Even though the shows made it look easy, I was convinced I needed more guidance to tackle the number of projects I had planned, and I knew where to go for help.

The local library provided how-to-do books with the step by step direction necessary to produce astounding results. I left the library with a stack of books and magazines that would teach me how to decorate, co-ordinate and accessorise every room in my house. Their glossy pictures inspired me to meet the challenge head on.

    I was interested in trying out some of the new textured wall treatment that would hide the flaws in our drywall seaming and decided to start with the bathroom. The books and the TV show exaggerated the simplicity of the technique as did the paint store clerk who made it sound like any kid in kindergarten could sponge paint. I arrived home loaded down with rollers, trays, brushes, sponges and four cans of paint to achieve the affect I desired.

    "Why so much paint? I thought you were starting with the bathroom?" Fred asked.

    "I am. One is for the ceiling and the other three quarts are for the walls," I replied.

    He left the house shaking his head and muttering something about an eight by ten room didn't need that much paint.

    I paid no attention to his remark and was glad I had chosen a day when he would not be home to transform our drab bathroom, into a nautical oasis.

I began the creative wall finishing by rolling a base coat of turquoise paint on the walls, followed by two shades of sea green sponged in a random pattern over it. When that dried, a border of waves crashing against lighthouses was applied horizontally around the walls and a fish print shower curtain more than completed the nautical effect. I emerged from the room, looking like something that had been dragged out of the sea and turned green on shore. Neither the room nor I came close to resembling the classy lady and the elegant spa that graced the pages in the book and I wondered if my nautical decor would eventually grow on me without making me feel seasick.

When Fred came home, he never said a word, just shook his head when he saw the tsunami that had hit our bathroom.

The next disastrous decorating miss-hap occurred when I decided to follow directions from the experts again and rag-roll the walls in our bedroom. Rag-rolling is a lot like sponge painting, but messier. I used two coordinating colours of blue paint along with a can of bright red for contrast. To my horror, the walls turned out looking like a murder massacre had taken place in there. Ugly wasn't even close to describing it. The nightmare had to be repainted immediately before Fred, or anyone else saw the bloody mess and it took several coats to hide it.

Stucco was used on the ceilings to hide the imperfections, but when Fred decided to go against my better judgment and apply it in thick peaks to the kitchen ceiling we were awe struck by how it changed the room's atmosphere. A stalactite cave was not the effect I had in mind for my kitchen, though. We tried to knock the peaks off using the back of a garden rake, but many of them refused to fall. The paint dripped off the remaining ones, leaving a polka-dot pattern all over Fred and the new, gold and avocado green, cushion floor. Thankfully it washed off easily.

Wallpaper was very helpful in hiding what was underneath and very fashionable in the 1970s. For the kitchen I chose a yellow gingham pattern with brightly coloured tea pots and plates scattered over the background. Wallpaper had come a long way since the glue paste had to be mixed in a bucket and applied with a wide brush. Now one simply had to measure the length of the strip, cut it evenly, run it through a water trough and adhere it to the wall. Nice and easy, if you had six hands; two to hold the bottom out from the wall, two to find the match in the middle, and two more to keep the top portion from draping itself over your head and ripping in the process. But no one told me in advance, what a nightmare removing the wallpaper would be.

The wallpaper I used in my son's room was too girly for his liking and he begged me to replace it with herds of galloping horses. I agreed the flowery pattern was a mistake and honoured his wishes, but first the unwanted paper had to be removed. Armed with a bucket of water, a sponge and a scraper, my stripper day began. Soaking the wallpaper down, meant soaking me too as the water ran down my arms and formed puddles on the floor. Still the backing refused to let go. Hours later, I emerged looking like I had been dunked in a bucket of glue and thrown into the paper shredder bin. Bits of paper found their way through the whole house and gallantly clung to the bottom of my shoes. But it was worth it to see my son's happy reaction to sleeping in his stable full of horses.

One of the books I read convinced me that theme decorating was the best way to beautify a room. I chose a fall garden theme for my living room, to go with the newly laid, orange shag carpet. A mural of a forest path in fall bloom graced the wall across from the newly purchased, floral print sofa and chair. The flowers were in shades of gold and brown on a beige background. It was a perfect partnership with the mural, I thought. But, I may have gone a little overboard with the arrangements of silk and dried flowers in containers and baskets on every table. I even had a fake tree and a macramé, hanging plant holder with ivy cascading to the floor. Dried floral wreaths and straw hats hung on the walls and door, while silk vines curled up the pole lamp. It was a botanical spectacle to say the least.

  A touch of class was added to the room with a corner unit, imitation brick fire place that Fred built. It had a hidden bar with a drop-down door. The interior walls were finished with stick on mirror tiles. They formed an optical illusion inside the bar reflecting many more bottles of liquor than were present; a bonus and a nice touch. And by the time this blooming extravaganza was completed, even Debbie Travis, the decorating guru of the era, would have poured herself a stiff one and so did Fred and me.

It was December 2, 1975, when we finally moved out of the rented mobile home on our front lawn and back into our house, even though the rebuild was not completed. We couldn't live like we had been any longer. The water hose running across the lawn that brought water to the trailer kept freezing up and the forecast was for the first snow to arrive the night we moved in. The next morning there was a snow drift along the inside edge of the living room wall. There was no siding on the outside yet and snow found its way through an unknown gap between the wall and the saggy floor boards. The temperature inside the drafty house seldom reached above 15 in some rooms, depending on which way the wind was blowing.

Christmas was only a few weeks away, by the time we got settled into our remodeled century home. Christmas was my favorite time of the year because I got to decorate again. Somehow, I always over did it, with garland, lights, silk poinsettias glitter and festive ornaments on every surface and wall. We had lost all of our old decorations in the fire, but I managed to shop for more. When the word got out that we had no decorations, the charitable kindness of those in my circle of family and friends astounded me. Not only did they find a new home for their excess, the magnitude of their donations filled many totes when the season was over. Fire, or no fire, Christmas exploded once again in our home as it always does every year and I wouldn't want it any other way.

DEMOLITION DERBY

When Ron announced he wanted to enter his late Grandmother's old car, into the upcoming demolition derby at the Brooklin fair, his mother thought he had lost his mind. She was not familiar with the motor sport, but instinctively knew it was dangerous.

His father though, was a little more understanding. He remembered some of the foolish things he had done, risking life and limb, flirting with danger, driven on by testosterone beyond the boundaries of logic when he was in his twenties.

"A demolition race, Ron? Really? Your Grandmother would roll over in her grave if she knew what you planned to do to her old station wagon," his mother said.

"I don't think she'd mind me having a bit of fun with the old tank before it goes to the scrap yard. She put a lot of dints in the car herself, so what's a few more?" Ron laughed.

"It's sitting up on blocks, has no battery or tires and hasn't run for a couple of years. The engine is probably siezed up. I can't imagine why you would go to all the trouble of restoring it for a demolition derby?" she asked, unable to comprehend the reasoning behind it.

"Because it will be fun and it's something I always wanted to do," he replied.

"But you could get hurt. It's dangerous," she pointed out.

"Oh Mom! It's no more dangerous than riding in a bumper car at the C.N.E. I have already checked out the safety regulations. The car will be stripped of all its interior fixtures, trim, lights and glass. Rollover bars need to be installed and the doors welded shut. The race is held in a dug-out pit. No one can go fast and only a little gasoline can be burned. Believe me Mom; it's safe," he assured her.

"And how do you plan to make all those alterations to the car, without any cutting torches or welding equipment?" she inquired.

"My boss said he would sponsor me if I advertised his trucking company, on the car. I can use his tools and he even offered to tow the car to the Brooklin fair grounds if I give it to him for scrap when the race is over. I can't lose with Grandma's old station-wagon. They make the best demolition cars."

"I think you're crazy, but if you're sure you won't get hurt, I won't stop you Ron," she said, handing him the ownership for what was once her mother's pride and joy.

"Mom, you're the best," he said giving her a bear hug and a kiss on the forehead.

Three weeks later the car had been fully adapted to the regulations for the demolition derby. It was towed into the fairgrounds, to the pit where the race was about to take place. His Grandmother's resurrected vehicle advertised the name TIMMS HAULAGE in orange spray paint on the roof and across both sides of the faded, original, avocado green colour. The back was painted like a prehistoric monster's mouth, teeth and all.

The sky overhead was threatening rain, and the pit was muddy from what had fallen during the night. As soon as the cars were positioned, the drivers formed a circle where they were told to obey the rules. No ramming the opponent's driver's door and no sandbagging or avoiding the action. If the car failed to ram another within two minutes time, it would be disqualified. They shook hands and put on their helmets.

Ron climbed through the open window of the station wagon and slid into the single seat that remained in the interior. He noticed a large fire extinguisher at the entrance ramp for safety reasons. He tried to swallow but his mouth felt dry. He did up his seat belt and gripped the wheel.

"Welcome ladies and gentlemen to the Brooklin fairs annual demolition derby. Gentlemen start your engines," the announcer commanded. A din of starters grinding, engines revving and backfiring, erupted from the pit.

Ron's parents stood at the fence surrounding it and cheered for their son's hopeful victory in this competition of driving skills or lack thereof.

The countdown began.

"Ten!" squawked the portable speakers over Ron's head. All the cars were lined up backwards, so they could charge towards their opponents in reverse and hopefully save the engine from fatal damage during the beginning of the heat.

"Nine!" the broadcaster's chant reverberated through the glassless windows. Ron scanned the crowd that was gathering along the wire fence enclosing the dug-out. Some faces he recognized, some he did not.

"Eight!" screamed the crowd, who were as colorful and unique as the graffiti art work that adorned some of the demos. But only one of those works of art would survive to be crowned the winner today.

"Seven!" blasted over head while Ron gunned the engine one more time. The thunder from the powerful V8 under its hood did nothing to release the tension tightening up the ligaments along his rigid spine.

"Six!" sang the wreck-em-race fans in unison, while he fought back the rising terror forming beads of perspiration on his brow.

"Five!" cheered the crash crazed crowd, as Ron's sweaty palms gripped hard on the wheel turning his knuckles white. He knew he couldn't back out now, even if he wanted to. It was too late for that.

"Four!" boomed out somewhat loader. Even the most-timid spectators were caught up in the mounting memento of excitement, including Ron. His heart pounded inside his chest as the countdown continued.

"Three!" they chanted, mesmerized by the intense thrill of witnessing the colossal destruction of several automobiles. Ron was confident that the tough old station wagon he sat in was indestructible, but he wasn't so sure about himself.

"Two!" everyone yelled in unison. An adrenalin rush surged through Ron's veins letting the thrill of the challenge become the centre of his being.

"One!" they cheered. That was why Ron did it. He loved the high he got from facing danger and conquering it. He took one big breath as the broadcaster shouted, "Go…!"

Squealing tires, choking smoke and flying mud assaulted the ears, the lungs and the clothing of the spectators circling the rim of the pit. Most fans were fascinated by the crushing of metal and the oddity of witnessing such colossal carnage. In a short-time there were only a couple of cars left that weren't spewing radiator steam or engine smoke and were still able to move. Ron and his opponent fought it out in the far corner. When the battle was over, what was left of his grandmother's station wagon was completely unrecognizable. It resembled a bashed in accordion. The frame was bent in the middle giving it the appearance of a sway back old horse, but through the glassless window Ron proudly held onto the checkered flag.

"This is for you Grandma.' he said into the microphone. Looking up at the darkening sky, he waved it proudly for her.

Instantly; a flash of lightening bolted to earth, followed by a deafening clap of thunder that sent the crowd running towards their cars. It also caused Ron to drop the flag. Perhaps it was a coincidence or perhaps not.

EVADING THE BLUES

I am most thankful for the resilience of the human spirit that rises like the Phoenix from the ashes of defeat and sorrow to lift us to new found heights of inspiration and joy.

To be alive is to be subjected sometimes to the negative side of life; to feel the pain of sickness, the heart ache of grief, the embarrassment of failure and the sting of regret. Those downward spirals of depression are hard to overcome when you are the one caught up in their spiral. During those time's I have great difficulty remembering that, this too shall pass.

There have been some occasions when I couldn't concentrate on the future or think of anything but the heart ache I was suffering. To break that cycle, I forced myself to take notice of the small things that occurred around me each day, acknowledging the good things that made me smile. I wrote about them in my thankful journal and later decided to write a journal for every member of my family recalling and recording all the wonderful times we had together. The journal would let them know how much I loved them and how much joy they brought to me. When I was at a loss of what to say, I would tell a lighthearted story about an ancestor or a family member. When the journals were completed they were given to the person they were written for along with a new journal for that person to write their happy thoughts and thankful events in. The idea caught on and I also became the recipient of some awesome journals written to me. It made me feel loved and happy when I read them and when I wrote them. It was the best therapy for chasing away the blues and I truly enjoyed being the recipient of such a personal gift.

I have been guilty of neglecting the journals that now sit in a basket waiting for me to pick them up and record some cheerful stories for each of my nineteen great-grandchildren. I have been giving all my time and effort to producing and publishing books for them for Christmas. This piece might show up in next Christmas book titled, My Kaleidoscope of Short Stories. It's not really a story but more a self-help article. Maybe its time for me to pick up the pen and return to the journals while therapeutically helping myself to evade the blues that February can dump on me.

There is no better way I can think of evading them than with a healthy dose of thankful journal writing. I thank God for giving me the ability to write down my thoughts and for the people I share them with. Life's good.

EYE CONTACT

My identical twin grandson's David and Danny had a bond much closer than most siblings. They were born, mirrored images of each other. One is right handed and one is left, but what amazed me the most was how they could converse through eye contact, without using words.

When they were around four years old, I bought a Paul Peel picture called, After the Bath. It was a print of the famous work that hung in R.S. McLaughlin's bed room but I hung my copy over the buffet in my farm house kitchen. The two children in the picture were facing the fireplace with their bare back sides showing while they were drying off. I loved the picture. It reminded me of when I was young and used to take baths in front of the fire.

When the twins first saw the print, they entered the room and stopped dead in their tracks. Their mouths dropped open as they gawked at the picture and then at each other as much to say, DO

YOU SEE WHAT I SEE? Not a word transpired yet the feelings of shock and amazement that I would hang such a picture on the wall was obvious.

"That's rude," David commented.

"It's not rude. It's art," I told them.

That too is mostly determined through the eye of the beholder. Obviously the twin's perception of the picture was different from mine. They thought I had lost my mind and they were both happy to discover by the length of their hair, it was girls in the picture, so no one would mistakenly think it was them.

The twins were a constant cause for joy in my life. I recall the day, I was combing out Dan's curly hair and noticed a few flakes of dandruff on his shoulder.

"Oh Dan, it looks like you have some dandruff, I told him," while brushing it off.

Dave who was waiting his turn to have his golden locks combed, looked up at me with serious big blue eyes and asked, "Grandma, do I have Davedriff?"

From that day on Dave became known to me as, Dave riff and Dan, as Dandruff, my funny and amazing twin grandsons.

Their imaginations were so vivid. They would play out the personalities of any person or animal they decided to be. Acting came natural to them. My imagination would take flight when I was with them, turning my refrigerator freezer into a magical place where Lego blocks could be turned into frenzies by just uttering a few magical words, like," Abra-cadabra."

Marching around the kitchen in a drum band with a pot and a wooden spoon or building a ramp with my cutting board to launch cars off, were some of their favorite things to do at Gramma's. Making a tent out of some sheets draped over chairs, or line them up and play train.

The twins were my first grandchildren and they taught me well how to be a creative Grandma. We did have lots of fun and we still do when we get together and reminisce those days so long ago.

FAILED ATTEMPTS AT MOTHERING

    Along with raising five children, I have, over the years, extended my mothering skills to include several stray dogs, a one-eyed cat and any four or two-legged reject that showed up on my door step. When it came to child psychology or animal veterinary care, I winged it, using only my misguided intuition to guide me. No wonder the children and the pets that survived my mothering, were a little unique, but very interesting.

    As for the children, it took me years to realize that I had unintentionally contributed to them lacking a few brain cells by putting skim milk instead of whole milk into their bottles. At the time I was following my doctor's recommendation. I suppose he never read the article that whole milk developed brain cells and skim milk does not. Well that certainly explains the outcome of my mothering techniques on the infants that I nourished.

Our fine feathered friends never did very well on the parental treatment they received from me either. One warm spring day, I found a baby bird that could not fly yet, stumbling about on the ground. I gently picked it up and carried it to the house. I found a shoe box, lined it in tissue and placed the little bird into its new nest. Then I proceeded to find some worms for it to eat. It died shortly afterwards. I murdered it by not chewing or cutting the worms up first. I also drowned a bunch of baby ducks. How was I to know they needed a ramp to get out of the rinse tub full of water when they were finished swimming around in it? I never knew ducks could drown, but mine did. The only bird that survived under my mothering care was a budgie who thought it was a dog, and I never even fed it any skim milk. Perhaps it heard about what happened to the other birds I had mothered and decided on its own to let the dog raise it instead. It slept under the table with him and ran around the floor all day.

   Sadly, our mother cat rejected the litter of four she had delivered in a basket of laundry, in my closet. I was so angry with her neglect of her young that I foolishly stepped up to the plate, knowing nothing about being a mother cat. I fed the squirming fluff balls baby formula with an eye dropper. I diluted it more than it said to on the can and they didn't seem to like it. They got more on their faces than in their bellies. I was worried about fleas and ticks, so I bathed the kittens daily. They never liked the bath either. Within a few days they all died. Someone said it was the bath that killed them. Mother cats, so I am told also lick their babies buts, so they can go poop. I failed again.

      I chlorinated our fish to death too. By late summer the water was so dirty and smelly in the outdoor water feature, we had installed in the spring that you could not see any fish in it. I thought a racoon may have taken them, so I decided to clean the water up with a little chlorine. The next morning the water looked better, but the fish were all belly up in it.

      When a mother skunk was killed on the road in front of our house, my children insisted I give the four babies that were left orphaned a saucer of milk each morning when they returned for it. They were too little to spray yet, so we were told. My husband decided to build a pen for them, but they dug their way under the fence and ran away before I could do any mothering damage. I was not sad to see them go.

  Some things did survive under my care, including a crazy budgie, a one-eyed cat, a couple of spoiled dogs and 5 helpless children. It still fills me with amazement that they survived my mothering.

FAMILY POSITIONS

There are certain things in our lives that we have absolutely no control over, who our parents are, the colour of our skin, our nationality at birth, or what order we are destined to fulfill within our family unit.

For fifteen years I reigned as the lonely, only child, always wanting to have sisters and brothers. That request was fulfilled when I was fifteen and my baby sister, Wendy was born. Through her birth, I learned how to take care of an infant. It's a good thing she came along when she did because by the time she reached her first birthday, I was married ready to begin fulfilling my dream of having a large family.

Our first-born daughter, Karen loved her position along with the responsibility that soon came from having 4 younger siblings. She was mature for her age, a mother hen to the little ones, but she also showed great compassion towards the elderly folks in our family and neighbourhood. She was destined to be a loving mother and nurse, choosing to devote herself to the care of the elderly. Because we are only 16 years apart; in age, she now says we will share a room in the nursing home together when that time comes, and we grow old.

A few weeks short of a year after Karen's birth, our second daughter, Heather arrived. She was born with a turned in eye, and tongue tie, both were repaired by surgery and glasses were needed for her impaired vision. Heather was a sweet child, but not well coordinated. She had more band aids on her knees and elbows than the rest put together. She seldom got blamed for any mischief she took part in, because being second born allows you to fly under the radar a lot.

A year after Heather's birth came our third daughter, Laurie. She was feisty. Her rights were firmly voiced and defended. It was funny to watch her stand her ground against her larger, older siblings. I think Laurie enjoyed being the third in line. The rules were more relaxed for her and she did love to push those limits. Laurie was a live wire and led the others in sports and physical activities. She came across as fearless, but her heart was soft. She liked things to be clean and tidy and hated sharing a bedroom with her messy sisters. She was destined to be a loving mother, that kept a beautiful home, and developed her own cleaning company. Even though her 3rd born status called for her to stick up for herself, she was and still is a very kind and giving member of our family.

Laurie's birth was followed a year later by our only son, Robert. Being the only boy carried with it a coveted position in our family circle. I had no brothers, so my full attention was on everything this little guy did. The girls soon learned to send Robbie in for cookies or snacks because Mom was more apt to give into him and of course they would receive a treat too. Rob loved his rank as the only boy and although I thought he'd grow up hating girls. The opposite was the case, thanks to his sisters. They taught him how to dance and that helped his popularity with the young ladies. Rob got along well with everyone, including his teachers. He brought home citizenship awards and tries hard to keep the peace amongst our family and at his work place. He loves being a Dad, driving a concrete truck and being involved in the dynamics of our family. We certainly do have fun together.

  Bonnie was our last child. The baby of our flock was born less than one year after we lost our ten-year old daughter, Heather in a terrible car accident. Bonnie was and still is the ray of sunshine that brought us all through the sadness of grief. Her bubbly personality and wit keeps us laughing. She too loves her position as the baby. Her artistic flare, people skills and enthusiasm for life made her a pleasure to raise. She is a natural Mom, a considerate baker at her place of employment and a comical member of our family.

  I am thankful to God for the 5 children, 13 grandchildren and 16 great grandbabies that all hold special positions on our family. I am overjoyed! My dreams of a big, happy family have all come true. I truly am blessed.

FIGHT OR FLIGHT

Eight year old Rose had been the brunt of much teasing and bullying since she transferred to my school, near the end of my fifth grade level. Mrs. Williams, her special education teacher, asked if I could walk home with her and try to keep her from being picked on by the older boys. Rose glared at me, not wanting to be babysat by anyone, especially me, the girl she told to f___ off, earlier when I tried to stop her from throwing stones at some kids who were teasing her. I ignored her hateful stare, and agreed to do as I was asked, because I liked Mrs. Williams. Those were not my initial feelings towards Rose, though.

Rose had a short, chubby body and straight brown hair that looked like it had been trimmed with a bowl on her head. Her faded, heavy cotton dress, hung lop sided off her shoulder and her long brown stockings had blood around the hole in the knee, exposing her scraped, battle scar. When she spoke, she stuttered pitifully. I felt sorry for her and gave her a stick of my gum.

As the days turned into weeks and weeks became months, Rose let her guard down and her funny sense of humour shone through. We became good friends, who walked to school together every day. Rose made me laugh. She always saw the funny side of our own behaviour. We shared our dreams, our doubts, and our secrets, but I was shocked when Rose told me something she had been sworn not to ever mention to anyone.

With tears in her eyes, she revealed her sorrowful past. Her mother had given birth to her out of wedlock. She never knew her biological father. Her mother now lived in the United States with her step father and four younger step brothers and sisters. Rose had lived there too until when she was 9 years old. That's when her step father sexually molested her. When she told her mother, she was surprised to be informed she could no longer live there and was sent to Canada, to be raised by her very old grandparents. She felt she was being punished for something that was not her fault. Although she was glad to be away from her step father, she missed her mother and her younger sister and brothers, terribly.

Rose had developed a tough skin. She was not a bully, but she never backed down from anyone, no matter how big they were. I couldn't help but admire her courage. She had a mouth on her like a sailor when angered. It did nothing to defuse a situation, only made things worse. Trying to keep her out of trouble was destined to become a lifelong endeavour of mine. As hard as I tried, I could not convince her, to take flight, rather than fight. The wild streak of defiance in Rose would blossom as she matured and take her down many rough roads, but she would always remain my friend.

Rose developed a soft spot for people who suffered from heart ache or financial difficulty, as she did. She understood their plight and would do all she could to help a friend in need. She also loved to dance and had the fluidness and grace of an angel. Fifty years after we met, we were still going to dances together. Those are my fondest memories of a friendship that ended when she died at the age of fifty nine. If an angel can be allowed to wear her halo a little on the crooked side, that would be my friend Rose. God bless her.

FOOD AND ME

  My entire life has been spent shopping for, preparing, distributing or controlling my food intake. Not only is it a priority to make sure my own pantry is full, I feel a strong urge to contribute to organizations that help feed the hungry at home and abroad.

  Perhaps I should blame my mother for this obsession. When I was young, she'd put a guilt trip on me every time I left food on my plate, by lecturing me about some starving kids around the world that would be thankful to have what I had rejected. Although I encouraged her to give it to them with my blessings, I failed to understand how eating the food myself could solve their problem. But just knowing about their plight gave me the incentive to contribute a small amount of money each month in support of that cause, when I grew up.

  What about the hungry people and children in our own community? They could use a helping hand too, I thought. So, the soup kitchen that feeds the homeless and down trodden got stuck with their worst waitress ever, me. I never received one tip for my pathetic service, at St Vincent's Kitchen. From there, I ventured to the food bank at Simcoe Hall where I became a professional bag lady a couple of days a week. Bagging up groceries for the folks who sadly required more food than they could afford to buy on their meagre income, is work I found most rewarding and worthwhile. It is a hard job and tiring, but when the day-old bakery goods arrive, there is always a tasty treat to replenish my strength.

Food is the hub of my social life. My family likes to gather around a table to celebrate any occasion, where we demonstrate with food, our love for each other. When gift giving is required, I have discovered that food makes an excellent gift. I have never returned or exchanged a tin of cookies or a box of chocolates yet.

My friends and I socialize over lunch several times a month. During those enjoyable outings, I tend to over eat, bringing me to the final part of this saga, the trials and tribulations of trying to lose those excess pounds. The weight loss club I attend weekly helps to keep me focused, but the gym, the pool and the walking I do, builds my appetite beyond what a rabbit would eat.

This lifestyle that has developed between food and myself will, hopefully continue to nourish my body, and my soul as it has so far, but perhaps just a little less.

FORGETFULLY YOURS

On my journey through life, I have found the senior years to be the most challenging and humorous. The potholes caused by sudden memory loss has made it a rough ride. Using wisdom to bridge those gaps can help, but sometimes there is no cleverness that can cover up my lack of memory.

My kids think I am losing it because, according to them, I am also afflicted with the annoying habit of repeating myself. I have a large family and often get confused about who I told things to. Consequently, I'm either hearing, "Mom, you already told me that," from one, or "Mom, why didn't you let me know about that?" from another.

I have always been slightly absentminded but since I retired my forgetfulness has blossomed like never-before. It plagues my daily activities far more often than it used to, I will admit. Like last Friday morning when I could not find my house keys, but when I opened the door, there they were, still in the lock from the night before.

Everyone I know in their golden years seems to be bothered with similar annoyances. My elderly neighbour left his car running in his drive way all night. He forgot to turn it off. I have also noticed garbage left at the curb for pick up on the wrong day of the week. Those random acts of blunder, reassure me that I'm not alone in my quest to navigate the senior years.

People's names like to elude me too, but I remedied that problem by simply calling everyone, "Dear." It works well for all those nameless, familiar folks I encounter along the way and the "Dears." on the receiving end; think I'm a sweet old lady, if they only knew the truth.

Sometimes I wonder if my brain got short circuited, because things I used to know like my age, postal code and pin numbers don't always come to mind when I want to recall them. I also find I cannot trust my vocabulary anymore. It has left me pitifully, speechless and dumbfounded, smack in the middle of a sentence, from the lack of a single word.

One benefit I have discovered since I have become a sage of wisdom is, it allows me to avoid being dragged into other people's affairs by saying wise words like," I have faith in your decisions", instead of giving them advise that can cast the blame on me, when they screw up. It also covers up the fact that I'm not interested in their problems anyhow. I have enough potholes in my own life to work on.

I forgot my Son's birthday once and he's never let me live it down. I was running a day behind, in my head. Sometimes I'm a week, a month, or a whole damn year out of date. To remedy this problem, I bought a modern digital clock that displays the hour, the day, the month and tells me the temperature in the room, as well. Without it I'd be in another time zone, for sure. I bet it was a senior who invented that clock.

I think the greatest aid I have in my house is the magnetic calendar on my fridge, where I diligently write down every upcoming event, birthday, appointment and luncheon. I also keep a small round magnet on top of the calendar that I move along as time progresses, to keep me in the present. A stroke of genius on my part I thought. All I need to do is remember to look at it every morning.

Even with all these precautions in place, there is very little help for someone who shows up at the bank wearing one slipper and one shoe. What happened? Was my mind too busy going over the errands I had to do, to remember I had two feet?

Packing for a trip can be interesting too. Usually I end up taking far too many clothes because I'm not very good at predicting the weather, but one thing I can predict is that I will be missing something when I arrive, like my bathing suit or clean under-wear. To try to remedy this problem, I adapted the sensible habit of making a list of the things I needed to take.

Lists are a great help. I spend a lot of time making them for everything I do, including grocery shopping, but usually, when I get to the store I realise the list got left back at home on the kitchen table. Even when I have one in hand, I can still manage to forget an item or two. Those items are usually things I need from the house cleaning or frozen food sections of the store. Seldom are they from the bakery or cookie aisle.

Missed doctor appointments are frowned upon as are late appearances at social events or classes. Keeping life running on schedule becomes much harder as we age. Perhaps it's because we priorities life differently than when we were younger. On top of my daily list of anticipated events and duties is nap time. When I am not able to have my nap, I have been known to fall asleep in the middle of a boring conversation, sitting straight up in an uncomfortable chair. Comfort is not a necessary requirement for cat-napping, it seems.

Yet when it comes to other areas of life, comfort takes the highest priority. Like foot wear. My feet absolutely refuse to be stuffed into narrow toed shoes or ones that have too high of a heel or no heel at all. If I do, the complaints of pain are far too extreme for me to ignore. They demand to be in comfortable shoes or they will rebel.

I find the golden years to be a slower paced environment. No one over 60 seems to rush around or drive fast like the younger crowds. Even so, the reason I was going someplace, can elude me.

I get side tracked very easily too. If someone interrupts a conversation, picking the train of thought back up can be daunting or impossible when I have already forgotten what it was I was just talking about. Chances are, the topic of conversation will come back to mind, in another time zone.

It is wise for me to choose the debates I have with others carefully and let their ridiculous statements pass unchallenged, under the presence of open mindedness, while the truth that arguments upset my digestive system remains a secret. I don't jump on as many band wagons as I used to either. It takes too much effort to be involved in things that likely won't change, such as, other people's opinions.

I believe that wisdom is learning how to use your age to get out of doing the things you never wanted to do anyhow. It's finding pleasure in watching others tackle those unpleasant tasks and rewarding them with praise for being so strong, smart or kind, while I relax in my lazy-boy chair. It's a class act that takes years to perfect and that is why people are usually older when they become wise enough to learn to use it to their full advantage.

Everyone, regardless of their age can experience senior moments. Those potholes can affect the way I dress in public too. When you see me with my blouse on inside out or my sweater done up crooked, you'll know I'm simply having one of those days. Just don't tell my kids. They already suspect that I'm losing it, but I want to fool them for as long as I can.

Have a great day Dear, forgetfully yours,

Julie Timms.

FRAZER CANYON RUNAWAY

To be classified as a professional truck driver would take far more experience than I had acquired, in the few months I had been licensed as a class A driver. I was still considered a rookie when my new employer dispatched me to haul a load of fiberglass camper trailers, through the Rocky Mountains. The unfamiliar trek of the Trans-Canada highway that winds and snakes its way through the mountains and canyons from Calgary to Vancouver had a few lessons in store for me.

Following the advice from some of the other heavy haulers who ran this route regularly, I waited until sunset to strike out. According to them, I could make better time at night than I could in the daytime hours, with the slow moving, sight-seeing tourists to contend with.

The C.B. was chattering away throughout the brightly moon lit September night, as the trucking convoys kept in contact using a lingo I found fascinating, but confusing.

Furthermore; I knew once I went on air with my handle of "Daisy Mae", that every one of them would want to talk to the lady trucker in their midst. I found it hard to shift gears, steer and hold a mike and opted instead; to just listen. As the hours passed many of the midnight cowboys had moved in and out of my wave length. There was one trucker's voice though, that had stayed with me from the time I had entered the Rockies. His handle was, "Blue Ox". He was obviously travelling close by and in the same direction. He seemed to be well known by his comrades and I gathered from eavesdropping on their conversation, that he was a logger who could map this road in his sleep.

      "Breaker, breaker for the flat-bed with the trailers on board, you got your ears on?" squawked his familiar voice over the C.B.

      "Ten four, Blue Ox," I replied, checking my rear-view mirror and seeing the headlights of his logging truck rapidly closing the gap between us.

"Hate to tell you this darlin, but my brakes just let go and I 'm heading straight for your back door. Put the pedal to the metal, 'cause we're in for a wild ride tonight!"

I checked the mirrors again and could see the reckless speed he was gaining on me, as if I was standing still. "Holy shit!" I yelled into the mike before dropping it and shoving my foot on the accelerator as hard as I could.

The long grade we were barreling down was also the most treacherous part of the narrow highway that twists its way through the Frazer Canyon. To my left; crag rock cliffs jutted high above my view. To my right; the narrow, pavement had no shoulder and plunged straight off the unprotected edge, into the canyon hundreds of feet below, where the Frazer River roared out its white-water fury. The pavement was marked with solid lines, prohibiting passing. Signs warning of fallen rock, slow speeds and sharp curves ahead, flashed past too fast to read, as I careened down the mountain's face, chased by thirty tons of logs on a runaway truck.

Not a sound came over the C.B., until Blue Ox broke the silence with a blunt, but direct order to me. "Run off ramp, half a mile ahead. Take it!'

My C.B. microphone lay dangling from its cord. I could not take my hands off the wheel to reach it, but I felt it was he who needed the escape route more than I did. I contemplated ignoring his order, but another look through the mirrors convinced me to do as he said. Only a few meters were left between us now, and my truck couldn't go any faster.

The run off ramp came into sight, but at this speed, I doubted I could keep the wheels on the ground. Perspiration beaded out on my forehead and ran into my eyes, stinging and blurring my vision. With white knuckled fists I gripped hard the steering wheel and cranked it towards the ramp. Although the truck leaned, and the load shifted to one side, it remained right side up and the logger behind me sped past like a rocket propelled sled of timber, down a bob-sled course.

Over the C.B. came another trucker's voice, informing his friend in trouble, "It's clear sailing ahead of you, Ox. We got the road blocked from Hell's Gate on. There'll be no traffic coming at you tonight, Good buddy. Over and out."

When my hands stopped trembling I slowly drove my truck back onto the highway. All the time praying the Blue Ox could hold onto his runaway rig

and not end up dead in a monstrous heap of twisted metal and strewn logs at the bottom of the canyon.

I picked up my C.B. microphone, wanting to give him some encouragement and thank him for saving my life. I felt we would have both been in grave danger had he not told me about the cut off ramp. He knew the logs he carried would have crushed him, had he taken it. All the emotion I felt inside just couldn't be put into words, so I simply said, "Blue Ox, this is Daisy Mae coming at you. I know you're too busy to talk, but the coffee is on me, when you get your rig stopped. Over and out."

There were several minutes of stone dead silence. I prayed that this experienced trucker would be spared a disastrous death, but my mind kept imagining the worst.

It seemed like an eternity passed before the air waves carried that familiar voice everyone was waiting to hear. Still a bit shaky he replied, "Ten four Daisy Mae; just a few minor problems...... Any of you cowboys want to trade me a clean pair of undershorts for this hunk of broke down junk?"

Under the playful teasing that followed this remark surfaced the admiration, relief and respect they all demonstrated towards their friend and fellow trucker, who faced accelerating terror and miraculously lived to tell the tale.

As for me, it was my first and last trip driving an eighteen-wheeler through the mountains at night. There wasn't enough money or clean underwear out there to convince me to do it again.

FRED'S INHERITANCE

In 1971, my husband Fred and his three brothers received a small amount of life insurance money from the sad and untimely death of their dear mother. Each of her sons found a different way to honour her memory with the $1,000.00 they inherited.

The eldest brother used his share to purchase a top of the line, hi-fi stereo-system and coloured television, in a long teak wood console. Not only was it a sleek and modern piece of furniture, that would have pleased his mother, it also filled their home with high fidelity music played on its 8-track system. At my house, we still listened to scratchy records on our old phonograph player and watched a black and white portable television. I would have loved a modern wooden entertainment center but, Fred had other ideas for his inheritance.

Another brother bought an avocado green stove and refrigerator for his wife. The fridge had a separate freezer section on top and was push button, defrost. I dreamt of owning such an appliance, but alas; I continued to have to defrost my old relic with pans of steaming water and an ice scraper, because a new refrigerator wasn't in Fred's plans.

The third brother bought a soft top, camper trailer to enjoy with his family. The following weekend, we rented a camp site beside them and set up our tent. I admired their thick foam mattresses, on the double beds that tipped out at both ends and envied them for not having to sleep in a sleeping bag, on the hard ground, like us. I begged my husband to consider buying a camper for his children too, but he wasn't listening. He had other ideas of how to invest his inheritance.

He decided, all on his own, to purchase a rusty old dump truck in memory of his mother. She would not have been any more impressed than I was. He named his truck, 'Leapin' LIll', and began a trucking company called, 'Timms Haulage'. Little did I know how much this business would change our meagre, existence?

Over the following years, the company grew and expanded to several trucks and some heavy equipment. We sold our little house and bought a larger one on a couple of acres of land, where we ran the business from. I looked after the office and enjoyed the relationships I made with the families of the men who worked for us. I often referred to my job description as a Den Mother for a bunch of guys, who never outgrew the sand box,

HI-fis, coloured TVs, campers and modern appliances all came to us in due time, along with the satisfaction of being self-employed. I somehow even developed a soft spot in my heart for our first dump truck," Leapin' Lill". She was by far the best decision my husband ever made, even though I never thought so at the time.

Fred's inheritance gave us all a new lease on life and I am positively sure his mother would have been very happy with the way things turned out and happy that he never named the ugly truck after her.

AN UNSUNG HERO

Gail Ranger was not only my neighbour and my friend, she was also an unsung hero in my eyes. In 2001 she and I started volunteering two half days a week at Simcoe Hall, a local food bank in Oshawa.

For seventeen years, Gail left her home at 8:30 am and drove to the Settlement House on Simcoe St. South, where she worked sorting food and stocking the shelves. Her job there was a physical one, but she compared it to playing store when she was a little girl. Some days when the donations were exceptionally heavy, her back would complain but she seldom did.

When the food banks supplies were running low, she could be seen carrying in bags full of the dwindling items, such as peanut butter, cereal and cookies. She collected bags to pack the food into and accepted donations on behalf of the food bank. Her reward was in hearing the squeals of delight from the children who accompanied their parents, when they discovered the big bag of cookies she deliberately placed on top of their groceries. Gail knew the world was not such an unkind place to a child with a cookie in it's hand.

    Gail's generosity didn't just start and end with the food bank. Her helping hand extended to me and a few other neighbours when we were on vacation. She became our gardener and all plants flourished under her watering and TLC. The gardens that graced the front of her house on Capilano Cres., ++ were always spectacular. She loved to share her yard and her pool with her neighbours. On a hot summer afternoon, the phone would ring, and it would be Gail asking if I would like to come over and play. She even bought us matching hats to keep the sun off our faces.

    ' During the rest of the year, she had the ability to make everyone feel at home by offering a cup of tea to go along with a game of Yahtzee at her kitchen table. Although Gail had a kind heart, she had no qualms in taking her winnings from playing poker at the senior's center or the slots at the casino. But she was always the first to donate to any fund raisers in the neighbourhood. She would support others by buying tickets for events she had no intention of attending. She was also an easy mark to children selling chocolate bars or cookies at her door. Even stray cats came to her for food and a loving pat.

The attribute I admired the most in Gail was her unpretentious nature. She didn't seem to be aware of the amazing contributions she made towards lessening the hardships of others. Nor did she like being recognised for the work she did. She preferred to quietly work towards the betterment of our community

Gail may not have been recognized as a national, Canadian hero, but she was the unsung hero who lived on the same street as me and I feel blessed to have known her.

When I read this story to my writing class, they suggested I submit it to the Governor General of Canada for their annual Citizenship Awards. I wanted to, but I knew Gail would not be happy with me. She hated recognition for the things she so willingly did.

Cancer has sadly taken her from us, but it cannot erase the love she spread throughout her family, her friends and her community. All who shared her generosity will never forget her. I am proud to have known her and she will always be, my unsung hero.

GRANDMA'S PHOTO

My mother's 80th birthday was approaching in July of 2001 and I wanted to do something special for her to celebrate that mile stone. There was little she needed or wanted at this stage of her life. Her home and its closets were full, and her health issues prevented her from taking extended vacations anymore. As I pondered the situation, a flash of inspiration brought forth the answer; take her on a walk down memory lane, beginning in the neighbourhood where she grew up.

I even contemplated trying to get in touch with the people who now occupied the house where my Grandparents had lived for over 50 years. But I didn't know the current owner's name and it had been 30 years since it had been in our family. I had even forgotten the house number on Coburn Ave.

I rummaged through the old photo album and found a picture of my Grandmother standing in front of her tiny frame home. The house numbers were visible in the photo. I sent a copy of that picture along with a letter to the current occupants of 858 Coburn Ave, in East York. I gave some history on the house and asked for permission to bring my mother onto the property as part of her 80th birthday walk down memory lane. I sent my address and phone number and asked if they would please let me know if they would allow us on the property one last time.

     The phone rang within a week and it was the current owner who was delighted with the information I had sent him about the changes the house had undergone over the years. He was enthralled at how my Grandparents had dug out the basement under the house, by hand, one pail at a time. They built an addition on the back and installed indoor plumbing. They raised 4 children in that little 4 room house.

     I also told him that my Grandparents had paid $1,200 for the property when they bought it in 1925. By the time it was sold in 1975, the yearly taxes were that much. He informed me they had more than doubled since then.

     The gentleman not only gave us permission to enter the yard, but also invited us inside the house. My mother and her younger sister, Shirley were both amazed when my daughter Karen, pulled her car up to the front of the home Marge and Shirley had been raised at. Inside looked nothing like their meticulously tidy mother had kept it. It also seemed much smaller than I remembered. The floor plan had been changed around so what had always been the kitchen addition to me, was now a bedroom and the kitchen was back where it had been originally been, in the dining room. There were building materials everywhere amongst the miss match of furniture and every room needed to be completed. It looked much nicer the way it was years ago. It was a bittersweet memory for all of us.

From there we toured the area, remembering the neighbours by name and the corner store that was the hub of the community. This was followed by a trip to Danforth Park Public School, which no longer existed. A new public school had been built on the grounds and no longer carried the same name. Then we traveled onward to East York Colligate Institute, loudly singing the old alma-motto-salute.

We're the kids from EYCI,

Bring on the whisky, bring on the rye,

Send somebody out for Gin,

And don't let a sober person in.

We never stagger, we never fall,

We sober up on wood alcohol,

That's the way we get you see,

Our onward to victory, Rah, Rah.

And that my friend was how an old picture led to a birthday my mother would never forget.

HARRY TAYLOR'S CHILDHOOD

"You have nothing to complain about; you have a mother," were my father's words anytime I uttered a complaint about the unfair treatment I occasionally received from my Mom, during my childhood. Shortly after my father's birth, his mother, Mary died from a brain aneurysm in her early 30s, leaving four children to be raised by their Dad, John Taylor.

John had made a promise to Mary that he would never turn their children over to an orphanage, like her father had done in England when her mother also died young. John knew how Mary had suffered being abandoned there with her older sister, Harriet and brother, Raymond never to see her father again. Later they were sent to Canada to the Barnardo Home for Children, and she was placed to work on a market garden farm at Holland Landing where she eventually fell in love with John. They were married and moved to East York where they raised their family of four children. The youngest was my father, Harry

Taylor. He was only three when his mother died from a brain aneurysm.

After the death of his wife, John remained true to his word, keeping their family together, but it was a rough childhood for little Harry, just the same. John did his best in the situation. He worked at the Toronto Brick Yard and when he got home, he cooked and baked and laundered all their clothes by hand on a scrub board. He darned patched and mended anything that had a shred of use left in it. Other kids teased Harry and called him, Patches for the shape of the hand me downs he wore.

The three ruffian brothers became big strapping lads by the time their older sister got married and moved away. Without any adult supervision, most of the time, the boys filled their hours at home alone wrestling each other and pinning little Harry down. He never stood a chance, but neither did the furniture inside their rugged house. John made most of their furnishings himself out of old lumber. It was rugged and stood up well to the everyday beatings it received.

"The first one up was the best one dressed," Harry said jokingly about living in a house with no mother to assign clothing to the rightful owner. New was not in Harry's possession very often throughout his childhood. Even the shoes he wore were resoled or repaired by a shoemaker after his brothers wore them out.

Meals though, were healthy and filling. Harry grew to be a strong and healthy 6' young man on his father's cooking skills, he had acquired while cooking for a lumber camp, in his younger years.

Harry's manners were a little rough around the edges, but a pretty young lady named Marjorie soon entered his life and attempted to refine him, but his Tom Sawyer spirit would still prevail until the end of life.

Harry's childhood was rough. Even though he was grateful to his Dad for keeping the family together, he yearned for the love of a mother. John was not an affectionate man. He never cuddled or hugged the boys. He did remarry after his children were all raised.

Harry, like his mother also died in his late 30s, leaving his two daughters, me and my sister, Wendy with a deep appreciation of how lucky we were to have a mother.

HELPING JAUNITA MOVE

When I agreed to help my flamboyant friend Jaunita pack up her belongings to move, I had no idea what an eccentric collector of oddities she was.

I met Jaunita a year ago at the food bank where we both volunteered. She was a colourful middle-aged divorced lady who adorned herself in brightly printed, miss-matched outfits. She also loved to wear heavy makeup, very gaudy jewelry and modern, spiked and brightly coloured, hair do's, but her friendly, outgoing personality attracted me to her like a moth to a flame even though I am the complete opposite. I try to avoid drawing attention to myself rather than stick out in a crowd I prefer to blend in by wearing plain, drab clothes and little to no jewelry or makeup.

Jaunita jazzed up the otherwise dull food bank by just being there. I enjoyed Jaunita and was happy to offer my help with her move from a two-story house, into a small apartment. I looked forward to spending time with my friend, who's home I had never been in before.

On the day of her move, she met me at the front door wearing a big smile and pair of green coveralls over a hot pink top and long dangly, feather earrings. As I entered Juanita's house I couldn't help but notice a specimen from her road kill collection, as she called it, inherited from her taxidermist father. It was a somewhat flattened skunk with its tail raised. She said it was her security against home invaders. Sarcastically, I told her that was a great idea and that I thought everyone should have a skunk guarding their entrance. Other random pieces of predeceased animals were scattered about the rooms or mounted on the walls, such as a big ugly fish and a moose head with enormous antlers.

  The glassed-in cabinet in the living room contained both Royal Daulton figurines and bobble head dolls, randomly sharing the same shelves. The dining room mirrored this eclectic effect with its hodgepodge collection of plates of Elvis, Norman Rockwell and the Royals scattered haphazardly over the upper half of the walls. Several racks of spoons adorned the kitchen along with a display of laminated, scenery printed placemats Juanita had collected from the thrift store. There were stacks of outdated magazines overflowing in baskets on the floor and stuffed animals tossed on chairs alongside pillows of every size, shape and colour. Containers and boxes full of craft supplies and memorabilia were neatly stacked in every available space on the main floor. Jaunita had been packing up for some time it seemed, but there was still plenty to do.

By the end of the day, I was exhausted. We had accomplished a lot and I felt satisfied with our effort as I looked at the now bare walls. The house echoed its emptiness. The movers were arriving the next morning. I left after accepting Juanita's gratitude with a hug and wished her the best in her new home.

The next morning, I was surprised. Sitting on my door step was a large gift bag addressed to me from Jaunita. I carefully lifted the tissue paper to discover, she had given me as a token of her appreciation, the skunk I had commented on. She mistakenly thought I liked the flattened, mangy thing. Thanks, Jaunita!

If a home invader ever breaks into my closet, he is in for a shock, when he comes face to face with Peppy LePew. Every time I open the closet I think of my flamboyant friend and smile.

HETTY'S JOURNAL

Monday November 9, 1936

Lifting all those pails of laundry water and bending over the scrub board today has taken its toll on my aching back. When I looked in the mirror, I was surprised to see how much older I looked than my 35 years.

I suppose all the worrying I've been doing about Alf losing his job on the buses, has aged me. The jobless rate is the highest it's ever been since the depression started, the newspaper said. I honestly don't know what would happen to us if he is let go from Hollinger's Bus Line.

On a happier note, I'm glad to see Marjorie, take such an interest in the drama club at school. I could never get up on a stage in front of an audience and perform. Marjorie is more outgoing, like her father. They are alike in so many ways.

Tuesday November 10, 1936

I have been up since 2.45 am. Shirley was so sick her fever sent her into convulsions. Alf rode his bike in the rain to get Dr Spence to come and see her. He says she has Chicken Pox and Bronchitis. I hope the medicine he prescribed works fast. I am worried. The last time I saw anyone that sick was when my mother and baby sister died from the flu pandemic in 1918.

Alf went to his mother's after work and came home smelling of booze. I was upset but too tired to fight with him. I made a casserole for supper that I knew he wouldn't like. He never ate it either.

Wednesday November 11, 1936

I never made it to the Remembrance Day parade or service. Shirley is not able to go anywhere yet. Elsie and Alfie Jr. went without us. I feel bad because I liked to go to honour my brother-in-law, Lenny who died from lung disease brought on by the mustard gas they used in the trenches in France.

I'm also feeling guilty about keeping the pregnancy to myself and not telling Alf. I will tell him soon. He won't be happy.

My father sent me a letter saying he will stay with us while he is in Toronto to attend the Royal Winter Fair, next week. I am looking forward to seeing him and hearing the family news.

Thursday November 12, 1936

Shirley is on the mend and showing great improvement. I am so relieved.

I am worried about my brother though. I think he is involved in an illegal pyramid scheme and he is getting others involved too. I hope he doesn't get caught before he pays back the bail money he owes us.

The Sheeny man was my friend today. He trade bartered a beautiful pair of figure skates for Marjorie for Christmas, in trade for a broach I never wore and the skates that didn't fit her anymore.

There is something not right about the way Marjorie is acting. She won't say why her hands are so chapped and sore. She doesn't seem to be herself, either. I hope she is all right.

Friday November 13, 1936,

There was so much bad luck plaguing my day that everything I tried to do went wrong. I dropped and broke the milk bottle on the kitchen floor and cut my figure while cleaning it up. A thunder storm cut off the power, and I had to rewash and re-wax the living room floor several times because people kept coming to the front door and walking on it.

  My father-in-law brought his new car over and took me and Shirley for a scary ride around the block. A black cat ran out in front of us and almost caused an accident.

  The truant officer paid me a visit and told me Marjorie had not been in school for over a week. She quit, she announced and has a job working turning socks at a sock factory. Now I know what has been wrong with her and why her hands are so chapped and raw. Lying is not something she does very well.

IF I WERE A GEM STONE

If I were a gem stone, I would be a diamond in the rough.

The diamond symbolizes strength and endurance. I am sure the trials and challenges I have faced in my life have helped to strengthen me. I am not polished like some of my gem-stoned friends. Nor do I conform to society's expectations as to the correct shape or size I should be. My interests and character are rather unique and undefined by standard measures. I'm a bit rough around the edges and not anywhere near as sharp as those who are crystal clear on their points of view.

A diamond in the rough would not be judgmental of other gems that had flaws or lacked luster. My own brilliance is hidden, even from me most days, but sometimes what appears to be dull, can sparkle in the right light. I have played roles in both of those theaters.

The colours of the rainbow bounce off a diamond, adding sparkle and beauty to what started out below the ground as a piece of coal.

Diamonds are seldom found glittering on the surface for the world to see. No; they keep their treasure hidden from sight. One needs to be intuitive to what lies under the surface in order to unearth their treasure.

    The child in me delights in the colours wrapped inside the diamond. They shimmer and sparkle like sunshine illuminating inside a soap bubble. They reflect by casting rainbows of light and they are symbolic of love when bound in a ring. I believe in love and like the tradition the diamond represents

    Financially, I'm more suited to a rhinestone, but they don't come in the rough, so a diamond I shall be.

JULIE'S DREAMS

Entering my dream-world is much like entering the warped and whacky stage set of Alice in Wonderland or The Wizard of Oz. And the characters there behave just as oddly, including me. In my sleep I sometimes have the unique experience of being a super hero that could walk without touching the ground, fly from building to building or lift a vehicle with one hand. Yet when I become frightened, all the super powers disappear and I find myself unable to run away fast enough to escape the impending danger, or yell loud enough to summons help. It's weird!

Most often though, my dreams do have a sense of humour involved, like the time my mother summoned my help to roll out pie dough. Why she asked for my help is beyond me, because she knew that baking was not on my short list of attributes. But in the dream, I rush to her aid, rolling pin in hand and just as it was in real life, the damn dough won't co-operate, so I added some cherries to it and voila! The rhubarb pie with cherries in the crust became a gourmet delight. This might also explain why I have such a hard time losing weight when my dreams sabotage my efforts like that.

Pie making is not the only thing I'm better at, in my dreams. Being a sex- goddess comes naturally there too, but the aggravating thing is that I usually wake up, just when the good part is about to start and try as I do, it is impossible to get back to that moment. So; I've never been able to claim that elusive Sex Goddess title, in dream land or otherwise. My mother though, is another story.

I will never forget the time I dreamt about her and Kenny Rogers. In this illusion, she and I went to see a movie with some friends. When it was over, I couldn't find her and I asked my friends if any of them had seen my Mom.

"Yes," one of them answered, "She is sitting in the front row, necking with Kenny Rogers." When I walked down the aisle, didn't I find them both entwined in a passionate embrace. I was so proud. "Yup that's my Mom," I bragged. When I told her this tale, she admitted that I had better dreams about her than she did.

I also have dreamt of many family members and friends that have died. Most are younger and healthier than they were in life. Those dreams are strange too because everything that occurs in them seems so perfectly normal that even being together after death, doesn't seem odd. But when I awake, I do have trouble trying to remember what they said because in my dreams, as it is in real life, I'm the one doing most of the talking.

Reoccurring dreams often find me and my late husband trying to fix up some old house for our family to live in. It is a beautiful old mansion, but needs so much work to restore it to its original beauty. We are extremely happy to be working on it together, just as we were in reality.

Our deceased animals that enlightened my life on this earth often come bounding into my dreams too. Those are the mornings I wake up with a smile on my face and a warm feeling in my heart that echoes the memory of their unconditional love.

Nightmares don't plague me very often but when they do, I can experience feeling of deep sadness, horror, or fear. Sometimes those feelings of dread can stay with me for hours after the terror flick ends. I have even made long distance calls to check to see if the victim of my nightmare was alright. Usually, everything is fine and I accept the fact that it was just a bad dream.

They say dreams are a combination of your past, your present and your future. Most of mine are so mixed up they don't make any sense at all. I even bought a book on dreams but it seems to interpret most of the nonsense I concoct in my sleep as sexually related. The lack of it maybe; but at least I can still dream.

LACK OF FASHION SENSE

During my teen years, I sympathized with the school girls that were forced to wear uniforms like those ugly navy-blue tunics. My mother, though, thought all schools should adopt the uniform rule. She said there was too much emphasis put on clothing, by their peers. It was her opinion that how a child dressed formed a division between the rich and the poor ones and became the main cause of teasing or bullying in the school yard. By wearing the same clothing, she believed that problem could be eliminated.

I didn't agree with her. What about freedom of choice? What about fashion sense, or individualism? I preferred to wear a stiffly starched crinoline under a circle skirt, a synch belt and a cardigan sweater set, topped off with a colourful silk scarf tied around my neck; than to be cloned in any uniform. Some schools didn't even allow saddle shoes or penny loafers, my favorite foot wear. Their students' male and female, were only allowed to wear brown oxford granny shoes.

I thought it was a dictatorship that imposed the rule that girls could not wear long pants or jeans into the class room. If worn under a dress or skirt they had to be removed before class and left in the coatroom. We were forced to abide by the dress code set by the school officials. Thankfully, the one I attended never went as far as to impose the uniform rule on us.

I also was clearly aware of my mother's feelings about the tough kids who wore leather bomber jackets with motor cycle insignias displayed on them. I was not one of those hard rocks, but I did rebel just the same. I bought a forbidden denim jean jacket and carefully embroidered the name Jewel on the back. My mother was not impressed.

That jacket became a thorn in our relationship until a compromise was met between Mom and I. After months of arguing, she finally gave in and allowed me to wear my cool jean jacket to school with my similarly dressed friends, but I had to promise I would not wear it to any family functions or to church. I agreed. It would have clashed with my frilly church hat and white gloves, anyhow.

Although I wouldn't call my mother, groovy or hip, she was moderately fashionable for her age. There were no cotton bloomers in her underwear drawer, no corsets, or stays. A panty girdle with a garter belt attached was the extent of her slimming lingerie. While most women of her era were attired in cotton house dresses topped with an apron, mine chose controversial baggy slacks and loose blouses. In the evening she wrapped herself up in a chenille house coat. She had a beautiful figure, but seldom showed it off in her choice of comfortable clothing.

I, on the other hand was very fashionable and chic, I thought. I wore my hair in curlers all day long, covered by a scarf, and preferred to wear my father's flannelette shirt as a sweater coat. She would shake her head and utter something about silly fads and crazy teenagers. Later in life, we would both laugh about my fashion sense, or rather my lack of it.

When my own children became stylish, they introduced me to mini- skirts, platform shoes and psychedelic, hippy attire including love beads and peace pendants. They liked boys in long hair and big hair, bee hive or afro styles on girls. Other than the hair dos it became harder to tell them apart because everyone wore faded jeans and t-shirts with words plastered across them. Some not appropriate.

Eventually they grew up and now it's their turn to wonder what their own kids are thinking with the fashions they covet, like body-piercing or dying their hair every colour under the rainbow and wearing their cut up jeans so low, their butt crack is exposed. Their lack of fashion sense often leaves the rest of us wondering, what sort of statement they are trying to make and why?

Come to think of it, their declaration of independent attire is not much different than mine was, just more dramatic. Tomorrow's generation will find its own way to express them self and rebel through fashion, just as I did in my youth and my children and grandchildren did in theirs.

LESS IS MORE

Much of my life has been spent chasing the elusive pursuit of losing weight I have held membership in several weight loss organizations and bought many books and magazines on the subject. Some of my attempts produced minimal results, but none could come close to the astounding outcome I achieved with an on line weight loss program I signed up for.

In about my 6th week of the daily regimen, I hit the wrong key on the computer and entered my weight at 100 pounds less than it was. It appeared that I had a 100 pound weight loss in one week. Before my astonished eyes, the computer screen lit up with colourful balloons, and congratulations for meeting your goal banners floated by in gay profusion. I was being celebrated as an honorary member, and offered a life time membership if I kept the weight off for a length of time.

Try as I did; I was unable to figure out how to correct my mistake. I had no choice but to wait until the following week to record my heftiest gain ever, the 100 pounds that would put me back where I belonged. I was certain they would cancel my membership and kick me out of their honourable club, but their response was yet another astounding surprise to me.

After entering my correct weight at the record breaking one week gain of 100 pounds, that computer demurely informed me not to worry, that it's not unusual for people to gain a little once they had reached their goal. A little weight! They call a 100 pound jump in one week, a little gain? I was astonished. It had taken me 30 years to achieve that amount the first time and only one week on their program. Maybe I should contact the Guinness book of records for the most pounds lost and gained in such a short time frame.

If nothing else, the experience brought much laughter into my life and showed me that less really can become more and vice-versa, simply by hitting the wrong computer keys.

LETTER OF RESIGNATION

I believe the time has come for me to resign from our company, but not without regret. Operating our own trucking business for over twenty-two years has been an interesting experience I will never forget.

Together we built the business from one dump truck to twelve and threw in a bull dozer, a loader and a backhoe to keep things interesting. We hired enough men to operate the equipment and I took care of the office work, while you tried to find enough work for everyone else to do.

I suppose the proper title for my job is Girl Friday, but that sounds so casual and pertains only to the office duties, not mentioning the mechanical work I was called upon to help you with if no one else was around, nor does it shine any light on the den-mother attributes necessary when working with a bunch of men who never out grew the sand-box.

The title "Secretary" doesn't ring true either, because a mere secretary would never receive the fringe benefits I have received on special occasions. I recall the year you said you were taking me sailing for my birthday in September and hauled me to a highways auction sale, where you bought me a snow plow truck equipped with a blue flashing light. And the Christmas you gave me a twenty ton, jack. Not many bosses lavish such extravagant gifts on their secretaries.

  The problem is the job classification of "Boss", doesn't define your attributes either. That word is supposed to represent someone in charge, who keeps things organized and in top shape; someone of authority who the others pay attention to. Not someone who befriends everyone in his employ, letting them use the shop to repair their friends and families cars, loaning them money during lay off season, or paying their fines to keep them out of jail.

  How this company ever stayed afloat with you and me at the helm, I have no idea. It started to sink several years ago, when the economy turned sour and poor health arrived. We lightened the load by selling off most of our equipment but we couldn't stop the turbulent recession, nor did we have the life preserver of Unemployment Insurance to fall back on. It was sink or swim! We did far more dog paddling than anything else.

The fellows who worked for us came into my kitchen early in the morning for a coffee and their work invoices for that day. The laughter and good humour they brought with them was destined to become a fond memory to our children who awoke to the sound of laughter every day.

This letter of resignation was never tendered. The accidental death of my business and life partner, led to the company being sold but, I consider myself truly blessed to have been so happily entertained by it during many years of my life. All those lads that never outgrew the sand-box will always be remembered with joy including the boss who wasn't. He was my best friend too.

LIE OR NOT

This pen portrait was written about a very famous person. Please try to guess who it is.

This famously renowned person is best recognized for his successful occupation as a gigantic manufacturer and mail order distributer. It's an enterprise that engages the talents of many tradesmen to fashion fabricate and assemble the vast variety of goods they produce.

In his private life, he chooses to live and run his business affairs from a secluded, remote area, far away from the public's attention. This is uniquely accomplished through the operation of his mail order service.

As a distinguished celebrity he travels all over the world, flying from country to country, distributing his products. Strangely, his wife never accompanies him on these trips.

He's well known for his psychic powers and generous nature, which enables him to abundantly reward those who are worthy of sharing in his stocks once per annum.

He is a super-star who has appeared as the main character in many books, plays and movies. The settings are usually winter time; the themes are generally based on good being rewarded and the conclusions are usually happy ones. He also has without a doubt, the world's largest fan club. Some even hold him in Saintly esteem; others begrudge the costs of his products; but almost all of us have done business with him in one way or another, at some time during our lives.

Although he and his wife dearly love children, their marriage is barren of them. They do have several remarkable animals to care for, along with a large staff of unusual and talented employees.

On the rare occasions that he is seen in public, he stands out in the crowd, like a colourful, bulky, clown. His taste in fashion apparel has remained unchanged over the years, along with his age and his jovial, triumphant laughter," Ho, Ho, Ho."

The Santa saga is the biggest lie ever told, yet it continues to live on. Why? Because there is a spirit within us all that wants to turn the fantasy into reality.

Most of us have made gifts for others at Christmas before. Whether it is clothing, knitting, baked goods, toys, family memorabilia or decorative items for the home, they were all produced with the spirit of giving to those we love.

Playing Santa fulfills a need in us all to be charitable, to be kind to the less fortunate and to give anonymously outside of our own family circle. Doing so makes the festive season so much brighter.

May we do our best to keep the fantasy of Santa always true and may your Christmas be a merry one.

LIPSTICK IN THE POCKET

"Oh no!" Stacy squealed as she opened the drier door and exposed the load of what had started the cycle as white clothes.

Her outcry brought her mother into the laundry room. "What the heck happened?" she asked while surveying the disaster. Bright red blotches were smeared on most of the clothes inside the drier.

"I don't know," Stracy lied.

Her mother reached into the machine and removed her daughter's favorite white jeans. She reached into the heavily smeared pocket and found what remained of a melted tube of bright red lipstick. "Where did this come from?" she asked.

"A .a..a friend gave it to me," Stacy stammered as she looked down at the floor to avoid her mother's eyes.

"What friend?"

"Uh... Emily, I think. I'm not sure."

"You don't know who gave you this lipstick?"

Stacy could feel her cheeks getting red. Although most of the girls in her grade eight class wore lipstick, she wasn't allowed to until she turned 15.

"Did you buy this yourself?"

"No Mom, I swear I never bought it. My friend gave it to me," Stacy insisted.

"Even if you were old enough to be allowed to wear it, you should never use someone else's lipstick," she scolded tossing the remains into the garbage container.

"What about my white pants. I wanted to wear them tomorrow?"

"I doubt if the lipstick will come out, but I will rewash them and see. They may be ruined for good. I hope you learned a lesson."

"Yes Mom," Stacy said. The only lesson she was aware of was never put lipstick into the drier.

Stacy was glad when the ringing of the telephone distracted her mother. She listened in on the one-sided conversation.

"Hello" ……" Yes, this is Stacy's mother" ……. "What can I do for you detective Johnston?" ……." Yesterday, at the drug store, her and another girl on the video surveillance camera." …… "No sir, I did not write the note for Stacey to leave school at noon."……."No, I do not know Emily Decker." …. "Yes, I will bring Stacy to the station right away Sir. "

The colour drained out of the young girl's face as her mother hung up the phone and turned to face her. She felt ashamed and wished she could go back in time and erase the bad choices she made yesterday. Now the consequences were about to make her life miserable for ever. She stood slumped over with her head bowed and tears spilling down her cheeks, swearing to her mother that she would never skip school or take something that wasn't paid for again.

"Let this be a lesson, "Mrs. Foster said again, this time with tightly pursed lips as she grabbed Stacy's arm and pushed her towards the door.

Silence filled the car on the drive to the police station where they had an appointment to see Detective Johnston.

Emily Decker and her mother arrived shortly after. Mrs. Decker spoke first. "So. you're the girl that dared my daughter to take some makeup, are you?" she said accusingly to Stacey.

It was the other way around, but Stacey said nothing in her defense. She was too afraid. Nor was her mother prepared to step into the conversation until she spoke to the detective and got the facts straight. They sat there in uncomfortable silence until a tall middle-aged man introduced himself as Detective Johnston of the youth division and asked the four of them to step into his office.

"I hope this isn't going to take too long. Emily has Cheer in an hour," Mrs. Decker announced,

"I am sorry, but I think this is a bit more important than a cheerleader class," he said, as he pulled out his desk chair and sat opposite the accused girls and their mothers. He had done this many times before and it took more time to separate them for questioning. He would if their stories were not the same though. The first question he asked was, "Why did you do it?"

"She dared me to do it," Emily said pointing at Stacey.

Stacey did not reply. She sat looking at the office floor.

"Is that true Stacey?" detective Johnston asked.

She shook her head in a no response. When she finally did reply she told the detective that it was her intent to take a lipstick, but she got scared and put it back. Then Emily slipped one into my jeans pocket and told me not to be such a dork. I decided I would leave it there rather than be bullied by Emily and we walked out of the store."

"The surveillance camera showed her putting the lipstick in your pocket. But let me tell you young lady, receiving stolen property is as illegal as stealing it. You are every bit as guilty as your friend here," he informed Stacey while pointing a finger at Emily.

"Emily never brought home any makeup. I don't think you have any reason to keep us here any longer, " Mrs. Decker stated.

"I sent a Sargent over to the school and had the girl's lockers both checked, Mrs., Decker. Stacey's was empty, but your daughters had several new unopened bottles of expensive perfume and makeup inside. We confiscated it as evidence. She obviously has been doing this sort of thing for a while. I am tempted to lay charges but to have a record at such a young age is a shame. So, I am willing to give you both one last chance. Neither of you can enter that drug store again. Do you understand?"

"Yes Sir. I promise you will never see me in your office again," Stacey replied.

Emily repeated Stacey's response, but before she was finished making the oath, her mother cut it off by saying, "Hurry up Emily, we don't want to be late for cheer again." She never even thanked the detective for giving her daughter another chance to have a clean criminal record.

All the way home, Stacey kept apologizing to her mother, but her Mom was from the old school and believed in being responsible for your actions and in punishment for your bad decisions.

"You are grounded for two weeks and the dishes are yours to do every night after supper," she told Stacey. "I don't want you hanging out with Emily any more. You two have broken the trust I had in you and until that is rebuilt, I don't trust either of you."

"Ok, Mom. I don't want to be friends with her any longer. She tried to shift all the blame onto me. You don't do that to a friend. "

"Another lesson learned today," her mother said, and gave her daughter a hug.

Stacey made a promise to never take anything that she couldn't pay for again, and she kept her word for the rest of her life.

As for Emily, Stacey heard she was arrested again a few months later, for shoplifting at the mall and does now have a criminal record. Because of the record, she was not allowed to join her cheer group when they went to the USA for a tournament.

That is only one of the consequences of having a criminal record. Stacey was so thankful to the detective who gave her a second chance. Too bad the other girl hadn't taken it too.

MY AMAZING COUSIN

  Twenty years had passed since I had seen my cousin Ken, but the moment my uncle carried his cerebral palsy son into my house, I remembered how much Kenny hated having to wear shoes on his feet, because his hands were twisted by the disease that crippled his body, but his feet were to him, the same as our hands were to us. Instantly, I knelt on the floor in front of him and began untying the shoelaces, while welcoming them to my home.

  When his shoes and socks were removed, he wrapped his legs around me, pulling me towards him for a kiss. Ken's face was aglow with happiness, because he knew I hadn't forgotten our childhood together, before they had moved away to Montreal. My life had changed so much since those carefree years. I grew up, became a wife and mother and followed my dreams, while Kenny now in his mid-thirty's, was still a prisoner inside a twisted and crippled body, unable to talk, to walk, or use his hands.

"It's so good to see you! I missed you. Did you miss me too?" I asked rumpling his thinning hair and sitting down on the floor beside him.

Thump! Thump! He banged his foot hard on the floor two times in response. That was his code for yes, one thump was for no, I recalled. The intensity was also symbolic to the degree of his feelings.

My mind flashed back to the fun we had as children when Kenny tried to teach me to use my feet as skillfully as he manipulated his. He could grasp hold of anything with his toes. He ate by holding his fork or spoon between them and raising it to his mouth. Try as I would to imitate him, my feeble attempts failed pitifully but always managed to amuse Kenny.

"Are you still a poor sport?" I asked poking him, with my foot.

Thump, thump, he replied grinning from ear to ear while poking me back, remembering as I was, the races we staged as children, scooting down the hall on our backsides, Kenny always reigning victorious, because he would think nothing of knocking over his opponent if she foolishly tried to pass him.

Suddenly, he spun around facing his father, and made some excited movements with his big toe on the floor. His Dad responded by saying," Okay, I'll go out to the car and get it." Then he turned to me and added, "Ken has something special he wants to show you."

He returned with a square wooden board that he layed on the floor in front of Ken. It had the full alphabet arranged in blocks and the numbers from 1 to 10. Ken's toes began to swiftly spell out the words he was never able to say. Amazed at his ability to spell, I watched, as he formed the words, I love you.

With tears of joy in my eyes, I hugged him as hard as I could. My marvellous cousin, who could do all sorts of things that no one else could, had not changed a bit, in my eyes. Without the use of his limbs and unable to talk, he learned how to read, how to write and communicate by using his talented feet. Only those who loved him as much as I did could imagine the joy that accomplishment meant to him.

A trip to Montreal the following summer, for my Aunt and Uncles 50th wedding anniversary, made me stand in awe once again of my amazing cousins accomplishments. Ken could no longer be taken care of by his aging parents, who had been his sole caregivers for over 35 years. He now had an apartment in a complex built for people with special needs. He shared this space with his girlfriend, a lovely woman who was unable to walk or talk and was confined to a wheelchair too.

The staff that looked after the place and helped take care of the residents, was mostly volunteers from the judicial system, who chose to do their time helping the handicapped, rather than in jail. It worked exceptionally well for all concerned. The residents seemed to understand the difficulties of not being accepted by society, and working with the less fortunate may have helped the young offenders prioritize their own life differently.

As my husband and I toured the facility with my Aunt and Uncle, they filled us in on the wonderful education system that Quebec had to offer handicapped people. That was the main reason they decided to remain in Quebec after my uncles retirement from the Ford Motor Comp. They stayed in Montreal for Ken. He was happy there.

 Kenny proudly showed me his electric wheelchair that he controlled by foot pedals and while we were there, his girlfriend had a staff write a note for the beer store and had taken off in her wheelchair to buy a case of beer. Ken was worried when she took longer to come back home than he thought she should. So he struck out to find her. It's a good thing he did, too. She had a 24 of beer strapped on the back of her chair and she couldn't make it up the hill. Ken got behind her and helped push her up it. I don't remember when a beer ever tasted so good. We toasted their future together and gave thanks for all the love we felt.

  I was overjoyed to see my cousin living such a fulfilling, happy life. Remembering it still makes my heart sing with pride for him, my amazing cousin.

MY FEARS AND IDIOSYNCRASIES

I have suffered from foot in mouth disease most of my life. I inherited it from my mother. Some days my filter simply stops working all together and whatever I am thinking comes spilling out unedited. It's like being under the influence of an embarrassing, truth serum and it has built in me, a fear of saying the wrong thing.

The art of using tact or diplomacy occasionally comes to my rescue in time to save me from making a complete ass of myself, but not always. I have played the role so many times in my life that I have it down pat. I also learned by watching how my husband coped in similar situations, by using his sense of humour to convince the recipient of his uncensored comments that he was only kidding. He laughed at himself. That was a choice he made every time he mispronounced a word or said something derogative to another person. He was very funny when he cut himself up and made a joke about it.

The fear of failure never bothered me or any of my family much. If anything, I was more influenced by an inflated sense of self-assurance. Meaning I was raised and so were my children to believe that we could accomplish any of our goals if we worked hard enough and believed in ourselves. To this day, I'm still naive enough to have faith in my humble attempts at being a writer. The paths it has led me down and the friends I have made during this journey are amazing. s.

Criticism though, can cause me grief. I don't like being judged harshly or criticized by others even when I know I'm wrong. The ones that I have the hardest time with are the hypocrites. Those who look down on others, for doing what they themselves have done. We all have our hang ups. Mine is a food addiction.

I eat too much in a day and I use all kinds of excuses and tell myself I must stop stuffing things into my mouth, for health reasons but it hasn't happened yet. I don't like the way I look but I do like who I am, and I try not to be too critical on myself.

I used to worry about my children rejecting me and I have lost sleep over harsh words that were spoken between us on rare occasions. Those rough years of raising them are behind me now. At this stage of my life, I would bend over backwards to keep peace in my family and now my children are adults I see the same will to keep the family ties strong in them. Rejection is no longer a fear. It never was more than a figment of my own imagination.

Abandonment is something that can happen when people age beyond the years of being able to remain self-sufficient in society. I worry about that but, I think having a pleasant attitude helps to keep life enjoyable no matter what stage we are at. It is my hope that a good sense of humour will follow me into my old age and that my size 10 feet don't end up in my mouth too often.

MY MOTHER'S FAMOUS WORDS

"Close the door, were you born in a barn?" Mom asked many times while I was a youngster. How do I know where the heck I was born? You'd think she would remember if it was a barn or not. Sometimes I wondered if I was adopted. She seemed to have no recollection of the place where I was born.

"Use your head and save your feet," was another one of her helpful tips that was meant to save the time I'd waste on making several trips instead of one. Maybe I wanted to make several trips especially if I was sent on an errand to the corner store on the other side of the playground.

"You'd forget your head if it wasn't attached to your shoulders," was her response when I'd return without all the items I was sent for. I had heard of the headless horseman, but I had never seen anyone walking around without a head on their shoulders because they forgotten where they left it. She wasn't fooling me.

"As long as you learn from your mistakes, it will be worth it," she would tell me when I screwed up. What did I learn from failing or making a bad choice? I learned how to feel like an idiot, how to handle embarrassment and how not to do it again. I'd rather not have to learn those lessons in life, but she knew I would experience them first hand many times, so she prepared me as best she could with her wise advice.

"Waste not, want not," was her motto. She threw out nothing that might be of use again. We saved buttons off old clothing and cut the garments up for rags. I was taught to bring home from school, the waxed paper and the brown paper bag my lunch was packed in, to be used again. We saved bacon grease for frying and stale bread for dressing or bread pudding. Sometimes I'd swipe a few pieces to feed the birds. We never bought wild bird seed, or dog food. He ate what we did, lots of leftovers.

The dog did not like the stew Mom cooked regularly and refused to eat it. I felt the same way, but was scolded for being wasteful and told about all the poor children in the world who had nothing to eat. According to my mother, they would be happy to have my dinner. "Send it to them then," I'd reply before being sent to my room for being cheeky. There I would contemplate how it would help the starving children, if I ate all the food on my plate? There was something amuck with my mother's logic.

"Star light, star bright, the first star I've seen tonight. I wish I may, I wish I might, have the wish I wish tonight." That rhyme was repeated whenever the first star of the evening was visible. My Mom was a great dreamer. She taught me to wish on stars, four leaf clovers, rainbows and lucky pennies I found on the ground. She made my childhood a fantasy of wonderment and magic.

I truly was blessed to have had the best mother in the world and I treasure all the things she taught me. Many of those gems of knowledge originally came from her mother and ended up being passed down to my children too. I hope they will always be remembered as part of our family's history of mothering.

Thank you Mom, for giving me a collection of valued information to draw on. I couldn't have tackled motherhood without using those same sayings when my children were leaving doors open, forgetting what they were supposed to be doing or needing a star to wish on. As far as I know, another generation are now being subjected to them too. Some things were meant to be passed down, but not your stew recipe. Sorry.

MY PARENT'S SACRIFICE

  Not all sacrifices made during the war years were comparable to the heroism of the battle fields, many more were humbly made back here, at home by the families of the soldiers who fought for the freedoms of others. I would like to share one of those stories with you. It is the sacrifice made by my mother and thousands of other women like her that kept the home fires burning.

  Marjorie Taylor was 20 years old when Harry, her husband of 18 months, joined the Canadian Armed forces and was sent to England. A short time before Harry was deployed, she discovered she was pregnant and eight months later, gave birth to a daughter, she named Julie.

  Being alone and taking care of a baby was not an easy task. Her parents managed to find her a house only a couple of doors away from their house on Cosburn Ave in East York. The house had no basement, no hot water and was heated by wood and coal stoves. It had four tiny rooms that all needed to be painted, but in no time, Marge had turned it into a cozy home for her and Julie. The only things that kept disturbing her was her nightmares she experienced at night.

    During the 3 years Harry was overseas, Marge was plagued with bad dreams about a uniformed man coming to her door in the middle of the night to tell her that Harry had been killed on some far away battle field. She was almost relieved when a letter arrived saying he was injured and would be returning on a hospital ship, but she knew not when or how bad his injuries were. Marge planned to meet him at Union station when his train arrived in Toronto. She anxiously waited for a letter disclosing the date and time for his return, but none came.

    Julie had never met her father, but Marge had his picture on a table in the living room and every night before she put the toddler to bed she would hold the picture in front of her little face, so she could kiss her Daddy goodnight. Pictures and letters were their only links to each other, but sometimes they were delayed by months or lost forever if the ship they were transported on was sunk. Many that did arrive had whole sections censored out making them difficult to read.

At 2 am, what began as a gentle rapping turned into an urgent pounding on Marjorie's front door, startling her awake. She could not find her housecoat. She wrapped the bedspread around her shaking body as she stumbled to the door. Peeking through the curtain she could see the outline of a uniformed man on the dark porch, reminding her of her reoccurring nightmares. Terror gripped her heart as she flicked on the porch light and opened the door. There before her astonished eyes stood her husband Harry.

"Oh, my God! Pinch me, I must be dreaming," she cried, as she melted into his arms in a kiss that embraced all of their love for each other.

Harry later informed her that his injuries were what they called shell shock and that he would be spending some time at Sunnybrook hospital while they tried to help him recover from the condition that affected so many soldiers. But what he wanted most of all at that moment was to see his 2 ½ year-old daughter.

Together they entered the bed room and Marge prayed Julie wouldn't make strange with her father. She turned on the light. The tot sat up, rubbed her eyes and called him Daddy, while reaching her arms towards him. Tears of joy and happiness washed over them. This little family was finally united again. Many others were not so lucky.

My mother's nightmares ceased as she struggled to help my father recover from the terrible things he had witnessed as a soldier. He never talked about them though, unless he did to the doctors at Sunnybrook hospital where he went regularly for treatments. Their lives would never be as naïve as they once were. Shell shock from the war had changed everything.

To all the men and women, including my parents, who made the sacrifice here at home and around the world, it is with deep gratitude I say," Thank You."

MY PET DISLIKES

     I'll often spend more time grumbling about the things I don't like than praising the things I do. It's a flaw in my personality that really irks me and causes me to rant on about some otherwise insignificant trivia, like the canned laughter used on certain television shows that are not very funny.

     I find it an insult to our intelligence when sit-com producers think we need to be told when to laugh by injecting canned laughter every few seconds during their show. Even good comedy needs a rest between punch lines. Ironically, the ones who abuse can-laughter the most have little humorous material in their scripts in the first place.

     Not everyone has the same sense of humour. Personally, I don't like slap stick or hidden camera pranks. But what I dislike most are people picking on others in a cruel or sarcastic way, or embarrassing someone and thinking it is funny. Funny material in my eyes is seeing the humour in one's own idiosyncrasies and silliness. It's describing those moments in a playful, light hearted or funny way. Laughter is contagious and will increase in a crowd without the prompt of the canned kind if the material is truly funny.

Another personality trait that rates high on my dislike list is arrogance. Nothing bugs me more than people who flaunt their intelligence while making others feel inferior or stupid. Not everyone is skilled or talented in the same way. Wise men say that the more they learn, the more they realize how little they know. I have also made the observation that as long as I'm the one doing the talking, I'm not learning a thing.

Bragging is also a part of arrogance that I find offensive, unless it's to do with some bargain I found. It's strange how my mind thinks it's great to broadcast to the world if I found a cheap bargain, but not if it was a high-priced item. I guess because one is bragging about name brands and quality, while the other is more influenced by frugalness. Both are bragging, but only one is acceptable in my eyes.

At the very top of my dislike list, sits gossip. I feel that respect for the privacy of others is no longer regarded sacred as it once was. Our society is so wrapped up in broadcasting everything from private to public information, that there seems to be no clear boundary between news and gossip. The private affairs of the rich and famous have always been sought after by certain magazines, but it goes beyond that spectrum now. Nosey folks can invade our personal lives through internet programs. Some will argue that fact, but it will remain one of my pet peeves that I try to avoid as much as possible. I can also see where the information given out on those programs could be helpful to thieves and conmen.

My final pet peeve is the number of times my telephone rings and it's a salesman trying to sell me something I don't want or need. The government has recently made it illegal for door to door salesmen to pedal their wears but have yet to ban the nuisances on the telephone.

I know that I would have a harder time writing a couple of pages on things I like. The negatives are always stronger than the positives, so they say. Go figure!!!

OUR WEDDING DAY
Sept 19, 1958

"They are too young. They will never make it," was the consensus of the small group gathered together in the little white, frame church to watch the naive teenage couple pledge their wedding vows.

"How could they know what love is at their ages?", the mother of the bride whispered to her husband once again, pondering their decision of signing the marriage licence so their sixteen-year-old daughter and her eighteen-year-old husband to be, could get married. The thought tormented her conscience. She felt her daughter had such a bright future until she became involved with that boy, Fred Timms. What did she see in him? He had nothing to offer her but a life of hardship on a labourer's salary. Even though the embarrassment of the pregnancy was hard on the family, she didn't have to marry him. They would have helped her but she insisted she loved the boy and wanted the baby to have his name.

Her father was not happy either, but he remembered what it was like when they were teenagers smitten with young love and taking chances that could have resulted in the same outcome, but didn't.

The groom's mother was no more pleased with this situation. She had let it be known that they needn't come rapping on her door when things went wrong. "You made your bed now lay in it," were her exact words. She knew the road ahead would be rocky and it upset her that Julie hadn't made sure a pregnancy didn't happen. In her mind it was the woman's responsibility to say no. Now her son was faced with a lifelong commitment to take care of a family and he wasn't even able to take care of himself. But he did look so handsome standing up at the altar in a navy blue suit, with a white carnation in his lapel.

The music began to play, Fred turned around as he watched his bride to be, wrapped in a powder blue gown and carrying a small bouquet of pink and white carnations come slowly down the aisle on her father's arm. Their eyes locked and a smile appeared on their faces. Colour came back to their cheeks and the ceremony began. Love radiated from the newlyweds as they made their way out of the church and into a life as man and wife that would overcome all odds and prove once again that young love can survive.

Together they made life's journey fun and filled it with happiness, babies and pipe dreams. Even though their wedding was a sad affair, lacking the cheerfulness of most, they would always look back on that day with the fondest of memories.

Not one person at their wedding would have bet a buck that the two of us would have made it, but we did for 39 years, until Fred's untimely death.

Would I do it all again? Probably. It was meant to be.

ORNERY CUSS

Public speaking can be one of the scariest milestones in life. Rather than allow it to become a stumbling block that could affect my daughter's future, I encouraged her to enter the public speaking contest at her school. To conquer her fear of being on stage she rehearses the speech she wrote on evolution, nightly, to everyone in our family, until we too knew it by heart.

Karen did well amongst her classmates and was thrilled when her teacher told her that she and another child were selected to compete with all the other classes to see who would progress to the district finals. The parents were invited to the event and I made sure I was available that evening.

Karen remained calm and collected on stage. Her pronunciation and diction were clear. I was very proud of her until the end of her speech, when she recited the poem called The Theory of Evolution from A Monkeys Point of View. It was supposed to read something like this;

Three monkeys sat in a cocoanut tree,
Discussing things as they're said to be,
Said one to the others, now listen you two,
There's a certain rumor that can't be true,
That man descended from our noble race,
Why the very idea is a dier disgrace,
For no monkey has ever deserted his wife,
Starved her baby or ruined her life.
And another thing you'll never see,
Is a monkey build a fence around a coconut tree?
And then let the cocoanuts fall to waste,
Forbidding any other monkey, a taste,
Or use a club, or gun, or knife,
To take another monkey's life.
Yes, man descended, the ornery cuss,
But brother he didn't descend from us.

Karen had practiced it well enough to recite it without referencing the paper it was written on, but when she recited it in front of an audience, she altered one word in the final lines of the verse and made her presentation unforgettable by finishing it off with; yes, man descended the horny old cuss, but brother he didn't descend from us.

The auditorium broke into laughter and applause, as did I. Karen smiled sweetly, unaware of the truth in her version of the poem. She never won the contest, but she did win my vote for being absolutely, right.

OUT OF MY COMFORT ZONE

Life has a way of never letting me get too comfortable before it throws another cluster of obstacles into my path. These unforeseen events can cause major upsets in the way I conduct my daily routines.

No one likes being forced into new directions, least of all me. At my age, having to set new goals, learn new technology or cope with new and stressful situations makes me anxious. I would rather keep things from changing when I can. It's comforting to know how things work and what to expect from the outcome of a familiar situation.

Sometimes when I find myself stubbornly refusing to conform to the new technology, I am left feeling out of date, obsolete and less knowledgeable than the younger, more adaptable members of our ever-changing society. To avoid that rejection, I have to tell myself, "Just do it," and break out of the comfort zone to learn something new.

Defending my point of view has landed me in trouble many times over the seventy-five-years of my life, But, I have noticed that it is only when I'm not in agreement with someone else that I am labelled as being over opinionated. Even so; there are times when I feel compelled to step outside of my comfort zone by defending the code of ethics I believe in. Often I just do it without considering the consequences of sounding off. That is why I have fallen victim to foot in the mouth disease more often than I care to mention. Now that I'm older and wiser, I'm hoping I will be anointed with enough wisdom to pick my debates more carefully.

      There were times when I willingly put myself outside of my comfort zone in order to say a eulogy at a friend's funeral, or give a speech at a wedding. But once I took the initiative to just do it, it was not as hard as I imagined it would be. Public speaking terrifies most people, but I find if I truly believe in what I have to say, I will survive the ordeal and even draw some pleasure from conquering that fear.

      Working on a fundraiser shook me out of my comfort zone every time I had to ask someone, if they would like to buy a ticket to help my gravely sick relative and his family. "Just do it," I told myself whenever I was in that situation. I did and so did many others. The sales of those tickets surpassed any amount I could have imagined and that would not have happened if the people selling the tickets had not stepped outside of their comfort zone to just do it.

We all must face uncomfortable situations in our lives. Waiting for surgery, going for jury duty and taking off in an airplane, are just a few of the many I have experienced. It takes courage to live outside my comfort zone. Courage I can't always rely upon, so sometimes I have to fake it and just do it.

The next time I am confronted with a difficult situation that I would rather procrastinate on than do, I will try to remember those three little words and "just do it." Hopefully they will work for me in the future, as well as they have in the past, while increasing the perimeter of my comfort zone.

PIGS AND PEARS

Living on the farm was new to us. Most of our lives had been spent being apartment dwellers. It was so nice to have found this huge two-story farm house for rent at half the amount we paid for a small apartment in Scarborough. The house had an enclosed sun-porch on the front and another utility porch on the back.

The one the back doubled as a laundry room in the mild months. That is where I did the families laundry, in the wringer washing machine and galvanized rinse tub on a stand. After the laundry was finished and hung on the line, the dirty water was taken by pail outside and thrown on the grass.

One day as I was busy dumping the water I was startled when the largest pig I had ever seen had gotten out of its pen and came running and snorting straight towards me. I could not reach the back door without going in the sow's direction, so pail in hand, I ran around to the front porch, with the pig right on my tail. In my haste, I never shut the sun-porch door as I flew through it. The pig came charging in on my heels. I was so frightened,

I dropped the bucket as I grabbed the door handle to open the inside door. My heart was pounding. Lucky for me it wasn't locked. I charged through and slammed it closed.

    Out of breath I looked out the kitchen window into the sun-porch and there she was, unhappily grunting into the empty water bucket. When my heart stopped hammering like crazy, I realized she was looking for food to eat. A pail to her represented food. Had I let go of the bucket in the first place, she probably wouldn't have chased me at all. But now here I was with a full grown upset sow in my sun-porch. How do I get her out of the porch I pondered?

    A light bulb went off in my head as I devised a plan. I got another bucket and put some dry cereal in it. I went outside and carefully waved the bucket in the open door way to get her attention. Once she turned herself around knocking over some furniture in the process, I stood aside and tossed the pail as far as I could away from the step. It worked. The pig came charging out the door and ran straight past me, to the pail and her treat.

This was not the only time I was called upon to outsmart a pig. The pear tree that produced delicious pears for canning grew in the barn yard where the pigs were penned. They loved those pears as much as we did. Trying to collect them before they ate them all was our mission. One of us would climb the tree and shake the branches to release as many as possible. Some of us would gather what we could before the pigs got wind of what we were up to and joined in the fun. We always left some for them to enjoy too.

Those were the sweetest canned pears I ever ate, especially in the cold winter months and the memory of how we harvested them is still ripe in my mind all these years later, thanks to the pigs.

PINOCCHIO'S LOVE AFFAIR WITH JILL

Jack and Jill lived in a house that Jack built at the bottom of a large hill. Although he was considered a Jack of all trades, it was obvious he was the master of none. Every part of the house was crooked, the walls, the windows and the roof. The roof sagged in the middle and there was a hole in it where a tree limb had crashed through. Jack had patched the hole with a red, metal stop sign. The interior of the house wasn't much better, but what annoyed Jill the most was the lack of indoor plumbing. Jack had started to install the bathroom fixtures and a kitchen sink but no taps or drains were present. She was sick and tired of using the outhouse and climbing the hill to fetch water from the well at the top. Every day bucket after bucket was hauled back to the house, but things were about to change when Pinocchio appeared at their door.

He was wearing a tool belt over his clothes and looked mighty handsome in it too.

"I've come to make you an offer Jill. I need a place to stay and I'm willing to do any repairs to pay for my keep."

"Do you know how to do plumbing?" she asked.

"Oh yes. I am a master plumber," he lied as his nose began to grow, intriguing Jill even more.

"It's a deal, you can stay here," Jill agreed, without even questioning his credentials or talking it over with Jack. She opened the door wide and let the homeless wooden puppet in.

Over the next few weeks, Pinocchio tried to attach shiny new taps to the sinks. While working the soldering torch in the bathroom, he caught the wall on fire along with his arm. Lucky for him there was a bucket of water beside the sink to stick his arm in and extinguish the flames. He threw what was left onto the smoldering wall. Then he covered up the burn hole with duct-tape and hoped no one would notice.

Pinocchio continued to brag about his imaginary talents to Jill and his nose kept growing before her eyes. Every time that happened she would become excited and want to kiss the charming little puppet with his unique anatomy. She couldn't help herself. He was irresistible and much sexier than Jack was.

Jill let him know how she felt and Pinocchio said he loved her too, but his nose disagreed. He did love all the attention she gave him when Jack wasn't around, though.

The two of them sent poor Jack up that hill for water many more times a day than was necessary. One morning Jill did something out of the ordinary, she went up the hill with Jack and a terrible accident happened.

The newspapers headlines reported that Jack had fallen down the hill and broke his crown. He was taken to the hospital in a coma. It seemed a little odd to the investigating detectives that Jill claimed she had tumbled down right after him but without a scratch. Only her bucket was dented in the shape of Jack's head, giving suspicion the idea that his fall may not have been accidental.

Whacking Jack with her bucket full of water and sending him tumbling down the hill was all Jill's idea. She wasn't interested in climbing that damn hill to fetch water anymore. She wanted indoor-plumbing, but Jack stubbornly refused to install it. Pinocchio on the other hand, led Jill to believe that he could do anything she wanted for a favour or two of course.

Pinocchio always was a convincing liar. Theirs was a fantasy love affair that may have gone on for ever if it hadn't been for Jiminy Cricket's interference.

That cricket knew when Pinocchio was getting in over his head. Jiminy also reasoned that if Jill had sent Jack to the hospital in a coma, she could just as easily burn Pinocchio too. Soon enough she would discover that the promises Pinocchio made wouldn't hold water. Then what? Soon after Jiminy Cricket put these thoughts in the wooden puppet's conscience, the love affair between Pinocchio and Jill started falling apart.

Splinters began to appear in their relationship when Jill realized what a mistake she had made in believing everything Pinocchio had told her. Without Jack around, she expected Pinocchio to run up the hill and fetch buckets of water at her beckon command and she continued adding more chores onto his to-do-list.

He kept trying to make excuses to get out of the work, but his nose would grow and Jill always responded to it in a sexual way. Poor Pinocchio was so tired out from climbing the hill, carrying back water, doing repairs and being her boy toy that he called on the Blue fairy and asked her for help.

She told Pinocchio she would go to the hospital and fix Jacks broken crown, if he left Jill immediately. He agreed and the very next day Jack was discharged from the hospital and Jill could not find Pinocchio anywhere.

The last I heard, Jack was taking a plumbing course and was giving Jill what she wanted most, running water inside their house. She is no longer pinning away for her naughty little puppet with his amazing anatomy and has promised never to whack Jack with a bucket full of water again. But to be sure, Jack makes the trips to the well by himself each day.

As for Pinocchio, the last I heard, he was hanging around with a senior's writing group in Oshawa and entertaining them with his fictional lies. He thinks he has found where he belongs.

Where he is appreciated for doing what he does best, making up stories.

REMEMBRANCE DAY

I thought about writing this assignment on the horrors of war, the atrocities, the sorrow and the ultimate sacrifice paid by those brave souls who gave their lives to defend our freedoms and rights, but instead; I choose to share the humbler sacrifice made by my mother and thousands of other women like her, on the home front.

Marjorie Taylor was 20 years old when her husband of 18 months, joined the Canadian Armed forces and was sent to England. Eight months after he was deployed, Marge gave birth to their first daughter. She moved closer to her parents and appreciated their help with the colicky baby she named Julie.

Marge was plagued with bad dreams about a uniformed man coming to her door in the middle of the night to tell her that Harry was killed in some far away battle field. She was almost relieved when a letter arrived saying he was injured and would be returning on a hospital ship, but she knew not when or how bad his injuries were. Marge planned to meet him at the Union station when his train arrived. She even bought herself a red wool coat with black velvet trim and hand smocked an outfit for Julie to wear to that occasion. She waited for a letter disclosing the date and time for his return, but none came.

    Julie had never met her father, but Marge had his picture on a table in the living room and every night before she put the toddler to bed she would hold the picture in front of her little face, so she could kiss her Daddy goodnight. Pictures and letters were their only links to each other, but sometimes they were delayed by months or lost forever if the ship transporting them was sunk. Many personal letters that did arrive had whole sections censored out making them difficult to read, but that sort of censorship was about to end for the Taylor family.

    What began as a gentle rapping turned into an urgent pounding on Marjorie's front door, startling her awake. She could not find her housecoat. She wrapped the bedspread around her shaking body as she stumbled to the door. Peeking through the curtain she could see the outline of a uniformed man on the dark porch, reminding her of her reoccurring nightmares. Terror gripped her heart as she flicked on the porch light and opened the door. There before her astonished eyes stood her husband Harry.

"Oh, my God! Pinch me, I must be dreaming," she said, as she melted into the kiss she had longed for since he left so long ago. They remained locked in each other's embrace in the doorway for a long time.

Harry later informed her that his injuries were what they called shell shock and that he would be spending some time at Sunnybrook hospital while they tried to help him recover from the condition that affected so many soldiers. But what he wanted most of all at that moment was to hold his wife in his arms and to see his daughter for the first time.

Together they entered the bed room and Marge prayed Julie wouldn't make strange with her father. She turned on the light. The baby sat up, rubbed her eyes and called him Daddy, while reaching her arms towards him. Tears of joy and happiness washed over them. This little family was finally united again.

I will never forget the sacrifice they made or the debt we owe to all the men and women who defended the freedoms of mankind and those who kept the home-fires burning.

SHANNON'S INTUITION

"Hello, my name is Millie and I'm phoning about the room, you have advertised on the internet for rent, near Durham College. Is it still available?" the female voice with a quaint English accent, asked Shannon.

"Yes, it is," she replied, amazed at how fast the internet worked. She had just listed it an hour ago. A clean furnished room with private washroom and kitchen privileges, good for student. Close to bus route to Durham College. Prefer female.

"I am calling you from England. I will be arriving in Canada next month and will be staying for 9 months until my course is finished. If you agree to rent the room to me, I will send you a cheque for the full nine-months rent," she surprisingly offered.

"There is no need for you to send that much money. I will be happy to rent the room to you with the first and last-months rent in advance," Shannon replied, thinking how odd it was to rent a room sight unseen but realized for a student overseas there was no other option.

"Oh, sorry, it can't be done that way because my housing costs are being paid through a grant and the administrator will only issue one cheque for the full amount to the landlord. Please give me your name and address for him to send it too," she explained.

"Oh, I see. Alright then. I will send you a receipt as soon as it arrives."

"No need. When the cheque comes back it's their receipt," Millie said. She never did disclose her address to Shannon.

Shannon ended the telephone conversation asking a few personal questions. Millie said she was 20 years old and lived in her widowed mother's small flat in London. A grant was paying for her to finish her nursing course in Canada. She gave Shannon a phone number in case she needed to get a hold of her and ended their phone conversation with "Cheers," rather than," good bye."

Shannon hung up the phone feeling elated to have succeeded in bringing in extra money to help pay the mortgage on the town house she shared with her three-year-old son. It was tough being a single, working Mother with little to no child support to rely on. The rent money would be a great help.

A week later the mail man delivered an envelope post marked from London, England. She opened it to discover a cheque inside made out in her name, for the total sum of $4500. Nine-months-worth of rent paid in advance, just as Millie said.

But; as delighted as Shannon was, she couldn't help thinking it was strange for Millie to be this trusting. She never even asked if Shannon owned the property. For all she knew, Shannon could cash this cheque and move away leaving her with nowhere to live when she arrived in Canada. It was odd. Shannon shook off the feelings of apprehension and took the cheque to her bank and deposited it into her account, smiling at her very healthy balance.

A few days later there was a message left on her answering machine from Millie. An emergency had come up and it was important that she talk to Shannon right away.

Shannon never considered the time change when she placed the call at 9;30 pm. She was a bit shocked when a man's voice answered the phone.

" Hello. Is Millie there please," she inquired,

" Whatcha doin callin here in the middle of the night? Millie won't be back till mornin" he rudely stated to Shannon's surprise.

"She left me an urgent message to contact her. "she explained.

"Give me your name and number, I'll have her call you on the telly when she comes in, "he said and hung the phone up the moment he received the information without even saying good bye.

When the call was returned, it didn't sound like Millie's voice at all.

"My Dad has had a heart attack and needs emergency surgery. It's not all covered by the medical here and I really need some of the rent money back. Could you please wire me $1500, by Western Union today and I will give it back to you when I arrive next month?"

Stunned Shannon agreed to do as she asked. But something still felt off about this arrangement. Then it hit her. Millie told her she lived with her widowed mother. Her father was dead.

She went to the police station and told the officer on duty what had occurred and gave him the phone number.

"It is a scam being plied on people who advertise rooms for rent to students, on line. The way it works is, they forward you a cheque for a large amount to deposit in your account. It takes several weeks for the cheque to be returned NSF from a foreign country. In the meantime the unsuspecting victim is asked to wire part of the funds back to the phantom renter and they are left holding the bag for that amount when the cheque bounces," the officer explained.

It's a good thing Shannon was suspicious and had enough good sense to go to the police before she was out the $1500 they asked her to wire. Hopefully those scammers were caught and put out of business, but likely, a more elaborate scam will be devised by defrauders to cheat honest people out of their resources.

SOUP KITCHEN

  The pungent smell of cheap wine, stale tobacco and body odor enveloped Gus as he leaned against the outside wall of the soup kitchen, looking down at his worn-out shoes. There were other destitute adults along with a few helpless children, slouched in the growing line up, waiting for the second seating to be allowed into the basement, dining-room of St. Vincent's Kitchen.

  Gus just missed out on the first seating by a few minutes and now he had no choice but to give up his spot or wait in the rain until those fifty regular patrons finished eating. He thought how symbolic this was to his life. Someone else always caught a break while he stood rejected, waiting for his luck to change.

  "Got a smoke on ya?" the young lad behind him asked.

  "Here, you can have the rest of this one," he said handing the half-smoked butt to his street companion.

Gus pulled his tattered, jean jacket tighter around his tall, thin frame and shivered. He ignored the people who passed by on King Street in Oshawa. Most of them preferred not to glance down the side street where the soup kitchen was located, on the corner. They choose to remain oblivious to the social outcasts standing in a line up along the sidewalk, as they scurried past trying not making eye contact.

"I hear the price of a meal ticket is going up to a buck and a half next month. Some charity, ehy?' the guy who bummed the cigarette said before he coughed and spat on the sidewalk. Gus didn't answer.

Word on the street was, everything except their welfare cheque was increasing. Gus received around, six hundred dollars from the Social Services once a month. He was lucky to find a room to rent for that amount, never mind feed and clothe him-self or satisfy his addiction to cheap wine and cigarettes. He hated begging for money, but that humiliation had to be addressed most months before the next welfare cheque arrived.

His way of panhandling, was to make a cardboard sign, asking for money and stand at one of the busy 401 off ramps, holding it up to the steady stream of rush hour commuters on their way home from work. The verbal abuse he recieved, was harsh. "Get a job, loser," was often thrown at him instead of money. His schizophrenia, mental illness and addictions prevented him from being employable. Gus was content when the passing cars tossed him enough change to cover the cost of a pack of smokes and a few meal tickets for the soup kitchen.

     His life was pathetic, but not as bad as the poor chumps who had no address or I.D. They were not entitled to welfare. Some of them slept in make shift tents under the bridges that crossed the Oshawa creek or stayed at the men's shelter if they were sober. Almost all of them suffered from one type of mental illness or another. On the scale of the homeless, the luckier ones were assessed as mentally or physically disabled and qualified for a disability pension that allowed them a few hundred dollars more a month to live on than Gus was entitled to. He had applied a few years ago for a disability pension but was denied it because the doctors said his mental issues were not permanently disabling nor was he a threat or dangerous to anyone else.

"Did anyone see Charlie and Sally go inside?" Gus asked the others gathered along the sidewalk.

No one responded.

Last night Gus gave the couple two of the six St. Vincent's meal tickets he got from a local church. He hoped they hadn't traded them for a joint again. Cause the last time they pulled that shit, the preacher found out and refused to help them anymore. Gus knew what it was like to be hungry and broke. Anything that could help take the pain away was worth it in his eyes. He tried not to stand in judgment, but so many others did, under the pretense of saving their charitable systems from abuse.

When the door finally opened and the patrons that had eaten during the first shift exited the building, Gus' friends, Charlie and Sally were amongst them.

"Thanks pal. We owe you one," the bearded young man and his pregnant girlfriend, said to their benefactor, giving him a high five as they passed each other.

"How's the grub today?" Gus asked.

"The soup was good and the rest so-so," Sally replied.

Charlie added, "The buns were so stale and hard, you could use them for golf balls. See you back at the rooming house," he said as they walked away. They lived at the same location as Gus and paid $450 a month for their dumpy rooms, but it was one of the cheapest rentals in town.

Gus entered the steam filled stair case leading down to the basement. The aroma of cabbage engulfed his senses. He never used to like cabbage but the luxury of being a picky eater does not exist when you're eating at this fine dinning establishment.

A small amount of the food cooked there was donated and on its best before date, or was the left-overs from the meals prepared at the local nursing homes. The rolls, cakes and deserts were all day old donations from the local grocery stores and it all helped to feed approximately one hundred people a night.

The commercial cook stove with its many burners and large ovens, graced the back wall of the open basement, along with a huge sink and dish washer. A wall of cupboards that held the heavy china dishes ran along one side and a refrigerated storage room along the opposite wall. A heated serving station separated the cooking area from the dining room. Round tables that held five or six chairs each filled the space between the support pillars. At the back of the dining room, close to the stairs was an open rack that held bags of mixed, day old buns and doughnuts free for anyone that would like to take one.

    The kitchen opened its doors early in the morning for the volunteers that prepared the vegetables, buttered buns, wrapped cutlery and cut pies or cakes for desert. When St. Vincent's delivery truck arrived, full of donations, they sorted the food and put it away. The cook and the administration staff were the only permanent employees. Churches of all denominations in Durham Region, were assigned one day each month to send volunteers to help-out at St. Vincent's. A few volunteers came from the judicial system to do their hours of community service required by the judge as part of their sentence. The rest were simply good-hearted individuals who liked to help feed the less fortunate.

The kitchen only put out one meal a day, dinner and that was served mid-afternoon, so that all the patrons could be fed, and everything cleaned up by early evening. A second group of volunteers and staff were brought in to serve the dinners and do the clean-up. It took a lot of hands to put out meals for over a hundred people every night of the week. Their work was vital to the poor and destitute of our community. Without them, many sad souls would have gone hungry.

Gus knew his way around the system. He knew where to go and when. The three food banks in Oshawa had formed an alliance where the client asking for help was only entitled to use their facility once every 3 months. They were required to use the other food banks on the in between months. Some gave out more food than others. Usually it was only a couple of bags for a single person. Enough to last a few days, but it was better than nothing. To qualify you had to show your income, your I.D. and your place of residence. Gus discovered the best time to go to the Simcoe Hall food bank was midafternoon on a Tues. That was the day when the truck delivered fresh fruit and vegetables, something he rarely got otherwise.

He took a seat at the table he normally sat at and waited several minutes before a plump wel-dressed lady with rings on every finger came over and took his meal ticket. "What's the soup today," Gus inquired.

"Vegetable; if there is any left," she nonchalantly replied.

"What? I stood outside for an hour to get into this dump and you tell me they don't have any damn food left? What the hell kind of a place is this?" he yelled.

"There is plenty of food left. Take it easy, if you don't want to be kicked out," she warned.

"I've been kicked out of better places," he replied, standing up quickly and letting his chair roughly fall backwards to the floor. Angrily he yanked it back up and sank into it. "Just give me my dinner, Bitch" he demanded.

Although he realized it was not her fault if the cook never made enough soup today, what annoyed him most was her, "I'm better than you," attitude and her obvious opulence. He felt like she was flaunting her wealth in his face while depriving him of a lousy bowl of soup.

      She took off towards the steam table. He was not sure if she would have him evicted or overlook his bad manners. When she came back with the supervisor, the place fell silent.

      The Supervisor was holding a starifoam carry out that contained Gus's meal. He was escorted to the exit and told to leave. Even though he apologized for calling the lady a Bitch, he was told not to return for the rest of the week. Four days without a decent meal was harsh punishment in his eyes.

      Rejected and muttering to himself, Gus walked the few blocks to Memorial Park and sat on a wet park bench eating his now cold supper while the drizzle and bad luck, continued to rain down on his life. Now he would have to beg for money whether he liked to or not or find some other way to feed himself. Maybe spending a few weeks in jail would solve the problem. At least they served three meals a day and gave you free room and board, but he squashed that idea because he didn't want to lose his room at the rooming house. It had taken him a long time to find one he could afford.

Maybe he could put the tap on a relative, he foolishly thought. None of his family was willing to loan him any money because they knew they would never see it again. He had accepted their charity many times over the years, but they seldom offered anymore, after he tore apart his mother's house, barricading himself inside because in his warped mind he thought someone was trying to break in and kill him. He had all her sharp knives arranged at every window and door, in case the killer got in. It terrified his mother. She no longer felt safe in her own home and she reluctantly made the decision that he was no longer welcome there.

After that episode, Gus had spent a lot of time living on the street. He felt he was lucky when he found a big piece of foam at the back of a furniture store and hauled it to an open veranda behind the Simcoe Hall food bank. He was told to remove it, but Gus had nowhere else to go, and after a few days, they threw the foam along with his sleeping bag into the dumpster. He lost all his worldly possessions that day. They didn't have to do what they did, he thought. He wasn't hurting anybody.

Although Gus had little faith in the system that supported him, he wondered if his social worker might be able to help him find a part time job, even though he hated the idea. He did not fit into the working crowd. There were others like him on the street. They were his friends, the social misfits, with as many mental issues and bad habits as Gus. They are a breed of their own,

After I saw first-hand, what mental illness can do to people young and old, I truly believe,' but for the grace of God, there too go I.'

TENT REVIVAL MEETING

My friend Rose and I were in our pre-teens during the early 1950's and highly influenced by the events that took place in our neighbourhood. One that made a lasting impression on me was the time Rose's grandparents, who were very religious folks, took us to a tent revival meeting.

The only time we had been under such a big top, was when the circus came to town and this event was destined to be just as entertaining. It was impressive and colourful. All the ladies wore fashionable hats, some elaborately styled with feathers, others made of straw boasted of wide brims and some were fashioned like a narrow hair band held on with a hat pin and trimmed in lace that could be worn over the eyes. Those were the hats Rose and I choose to wear, but I chose not to lower the netting over my glasses. I wanted to see everything clearly. We were both decked out in our best party dresses, white bobby socks and black shiny, Patten leather shoes. Our young bodies were going through that awkward stage between childhood and teens, not fully developed physically or psychologically, but ready for whatever the evening had in store. We would not be disappointed.

When Roses grandparents extended the invitation to me, I was a little reluctant to accept it. Not that Rose or I were unreligious. We spent several nights a week at various churches in our neighbourhood that offered young people's groups, C.G.I.T., or Guides. We enjoyed the slide shows at the Gospel Hall and learned how to embroider and knit there too. I attended a few candle light Christmas Eve service with my Catholic friends, was given a New Testament Bible for memorizing some verses at the Baptist Church and played the Virgin Mary in the Christmas pageant at the United. Neither Rose nor I ever missed out on a Sunday school picnic at Center Island, in fact; we usually got to go there more than once a summer, if we played our church cards right. The only reason we talked about not going to the tent revival meeting was because we thought church service itself was boring, but that opinion was about to be changed by the Holy Rollers themselves.

As the tent filled with people of all ages and ethnic background, the band on stage began playing some lively hymns and the speakers overhead boomed out their mesmerizing rhythm. People started swaying and singing along, including Rose and me. Our heads became swivels as we watched the congregation members all around us get to their feet and dance in the aisles. Not to be left out, we joined the Conga line. This was the first time we danced in public and the beginning of a love for it that would last a life time.

As the night went on, the waves of praise rang throughout the tent like echoes. We soon learned where to throw out a Hallelujah and when not to. Roses' Grandparents were very impressed with our interaction and encouraged us to join the Conga line heading for the stage where the minister put his hand on our forehead and told us we were healed. We didn't even know we were sick.

As naive as I was back then, the influence the churches had on my life was remarkable. I grew up very tolerant of everyone's right to worship in their own way and to attend the church of their choice. Today, my religious convictions tend to lean more towards the

Salvation Army, where my parents were active members. Perhaps because the music they play is every bit as lively as it was years ago when I attended the Evangelist's tent revival meeting with Rose and her grandparents and I will always cherish that memory.

THE APPLE NEVER FALLS FAR FROM THE TREE

As fate would have it, Ann, a head strong teenager was about to learn one of life's lessons, not taught in any school class room. Ann was a naive sixteen-year-old, when she became involved with a nineteen-year-old motorcycle club member, who her parents absolutely forbid her to go out with. She chose to rebel against their strict rules and continued to secretly see Boomer, the leader of the pack. Caught between her parent's harsh rules and the freedom of racing down the highway on the back of a Harley with the wind in her hair, Ann foolishly made her decision. She left her parent's home and moved into a dumpy rooming house with her wild but desirable boyfriend. Determined to change her parent's dim view of him, she tried, unsuccessfully to refine Boomer's crude manners and ways.

Expecting a baby was the life altering dilemma that changed everything. Finishing high school was no longer in her plans, but neither was living in a noisy, dirty, rooming house with an infant. Getting a job of any kind at her age, without having any training or experience was next to impossible. She lucked out and was hired part time by a minimum paying hamburger joint. Her part time wages were not enough to pay the rent and buy their food. She was forced to accept help from the social services. Ann found that degrading. If the tattooed boyfriend, with the Mohawk haircut had any intentions of contributing at all, he never showed it. Just collecting the welfare cheque, buying beer and pot, having sex, or riding around on his motorcycle satisfied his needs. Knowing she would be completely on her own, if he left, she resigned herself to put up with his drunkenness and verbal abuse. Lately, though, she kept contemplating asking her parents for help, until she finally mustered up the courage to dial their number.

  Making that call was humiliating because Ann had to admit, they were right, her boyfriend was a dead beat, jerk and she swore she wanted to end the relationship with him for good. Not until she was back in their home did she tell them about her pregnancy. Obviously, they were upset, but let her decide what would be the best outcome for the baby and for herself.

Putting the baby up for adoption seemed to be the right thing to do, but Ann wasn't sure that she wanted total strangers raising him. Quite a lot of time was spent looking into the adoption agencies. Relying on them wasn't necessary though, because a second cousin, who couldn't have children, begged Ann to allow her and her husband to adopt the baby, and she agreed, with a few stipulations. One of them was that on his 18th birthday he would be told that she was his maternal mother and it would be up to him if he wanted to have a relationship with her or not.

The months passed quickly and on an early spring morning, her son was born. Until that day, Ann had never experienced the depths of love that was placed in her arms, that day. As hard as this would be, she put her Son's welfare ahead of her own and handed him over to his new mother. Vanished were her doubts, as she placed him into the loving arms of his adopted mother and father. Wiping tears of joy and sorrow, from their eyes, they promised to raise him to the best of their ability. X marked the spot on the adoption papers where she signed.

Years rolled by until a few days after his 18th birthday, Ann received the phone call she was longing for, from her son asking if they could finally meet each other. Zero hour arrived as she nervously watched the motorcycle roar up her driveway and a leather clad young rebel, draped in chains re-entered her life, just as fate had intended.

THE BLACK DONNELLY AND CURSE

The massacre of the Donnelly family, took place in a rural area called Lucan, formally known as Marysville, near London Ontario, on February 4, 1880. The Donnelly family was annihilated by twenty of their neighbours who came to the home late at night to carry out the murders. During the blood bath, Johanna Donnelly cursed those who were killing her family even as she was being clubbed to death. Some say her curse was fulfilled with the violent deaths of each of their attackers, just as she vowed.

The feud began shortly after the Donnelly's emigrated from Tipperary Ireland where Jim was known as a brawler and scoundrel. They, like two million others were escaping death by starvation brought on by the potato famine. The Donnelly's arrived in Lucan and took up squatter rights on a 100-acre tract of land on the Roman Line owned by an absent Land Lord who wasn't aware of the pillage when he leased the land to Patrick Farrell, a farmer and black smith. Farrell made the mistake of trying to evict the Donnelly's from the land they had maintained for two years and built a house on. Jim Donnelly gave Smitty Farrow a thorough beating, lighting the fuse to a thirty-three-year feud that would follow. The community also viewed the Donnelly family as a pack of thieves, stealing another man's land. A court case was judgment awarded 50 acres in squatter's rights to the Donnelly's and 50 to Farrell. The hatred between them grew as time went by.

James and Johannah Donnelly had seven sons. The boys were as rowdy as their father and soon acquired as bad of a reputation that labeled this area as a gangster haven. The Donnelly's lack of popularity would take on deeper hatred after Jim Donnelly killed his neighbour and enemy, Patrick Farrell by hitting him on the head with a tool when the two of them brawled at a barn raising.

Jim stayed on the lam throughout the summer of 1857 hiding out in the wooded section on his own land at night and working the fields in the day, dressed in his wife's clothes and bonnet. After Johannah gave birth to their eighth child, their only girl, Jim gave himself up to the law, hoping for a light sentence because it was Farrell who threw the first blows at the barn raising.

The trial took place in Goderich Ontario. Jim was found guilty of murder and sentenced to be hanged. Johannah on the advice of a lawyer got a petition signed by enough people to have his sentence commuted to seven years in Kingston penitentiary instead. While he was incarcerated, Johannah raised the boys to be tough and stand their ground. She encouraged the lads to never back down from a fight. They were soon labelled the Black Donnellys because of their tempers. They also became prime suspects in any crimes committed in the region.

Soon Lucan was given the title of the wildest spot in Canada with vandalism, in full swing, crops destroyed, street brawls and cattle being poisoned and almost always one or more of the Donnelly boys were accused.

When Jim was released from prison, the family began taking revenge against the men who had testified against him in court. More property was destroyed, more lives lost, and the saga continues until the Donnelly family was massacred in their home in that vengeful raid on Feb 4, 1880.

The saga says, to this day, it is impossible to get a horse to go by the old Donnelly place after midnight, because the area is still cursed. A museum has now been built in the town of Lucan to remember the most violent family ever to settle in Canada, the Black Donnelly's.

THE HOUSE FIRE AND THE BUTTON HOOK BOOT

The shabby, insole-brick, clad farm house had stood empty for some time, inhabited only by field mice, before we bought it in June of 1975 and attempted to make it into a home for our family of six. We were very optimistic.

The century old house was well under renovations by the evening of August 27, when around two am, the sounds of crackling in the walls woke, 14-year-old Laurie. She thought what she was hearing were mice making a racket, so she reached out and hit the wall beside her bed, to frighten them away. The air seemed to be tainted with the peculiar odor and she wondered who was burning toast this late at night. Laurie turned her face into her pillow, but it too smelled like burnt toast. Reluctantly she opened her eyes and turned on the lamp on the night-stand between her sister Karen's bed and hers. The light illuminated the thick smoke that was rolling up the slope of their upstairs bed room ceiling.

Laurie's heart was pounding. Gasping for air, she pushed her 16-year-old sister Karen, out of her bed, to wake her. Terrified in fear and choking on the smoke, they quickly made their way into their younger sisters and brother's bed rooms, but four-year-old Bonnie was not in her bed. Panic set in and Karen refused to go down the smoke engulfed staircase until she found her.

Laurie and 12- year -old Robbie along with his friend Johnny, who had slept over, descended to the main floor while wiping stinging tears off their eyes with their pajama sleeves. Their raspy cries of," FIRE.. FIRE... The house is on fire!" woke their Dad and me and Bonnie who had a bad dream and had climbed into bed with us a couple of hours earlier.

Laurie immediately ran back to the stairway. In her dry cracked voice, she yelled as loud as she could to Karen," Bonnie's safe! She's down here with Mom and Dad."

Karen was nearly overcome with smoke inhalation as she half staggered and half fell down the stair case, relieved that her baby sister was not hiding in a closet or under a bed, as she had thought.

I guided the children towards the front door while Fred called the fire department. It was a night of re-evaluating and prioritizing our lives. Every one of us knew that our most valuable possessions were standing beside us, barefoot on the cold, wet grass.

The firemen tried throughout the night to control the flames and by day break had won their battle. The strongly constructed thick walls and massive beams of the one hundred and fifty-year-old house were still standing. They were severely charred by the electrical fire and the roof was burnt through. There was no way we could continue to live in the blackened smelly structure. It needed to be demolished or completely rebuilt.

A lack of fire insurance money, forced us to rebuild the dilapidated, old homestead ourselves and that led to the discovery of a hidden treasure. For over a century a small child's button hook boot had mysteriously been concealed between its walls. This obsolete boot was part of its heritage.

It had been placed there by the original builders of the homestead, at 1579, Baseline Rd, in Courtice, Ontario. Through research, I discovered, they, like my ancestors, were United Empire Loyalists. They arrived on the shores of Darlington Township, in the late 1700s, by big flat bottom boats. With only the crudest of tools, along with a horse or oxen, they began the back-breaking task of clearing the land and building their shelter. In comparison; we only had to clear away the fire debris before we could rebuild.

    While cleaning out the basement, we examined the 3-foot-thick foundation walls. Those heavy stones had been dragged from the surrounding fields and laboriously laid and cemented into place. Above our heads stretched the foot square beams that were once great pine trees felled by a cross cut saw and dragged from the woods by team of oxen or horses to be squared by axes, chisels and planes. The beams were then lifted by pulleys and ropes, and fastened together with wooden pegs, pounded into place by the muscle blows of a sledge hammer. The house was built like a barn. Thick, rough planks flanked its outer walls, rising vertically to the roof, and attached to the beam frame with square nails.

Attempting to rebuild the house by using the same quality of lumber as the original structure was constructed with, would have been impossible and far too expensive today. The outer walls were so thick; a chain saw was required to cut out the larger window openings we wanted.

In the true pioneer spirit, Fred and I, with the help of our family and friends, tackled the massive job of rebuilding but with a deeper respect and admiration for what the original owners went through over a century before. Finding the boot was like holding a piece of the past, in my hand.

An article published in the newspaper, by Bata Shoes reported that it was a common practice to place a shoe in the wall, during the 19th century. Shoes were considered good luck and would ward off evil spirits.

The boot now sits on a small shelf inside my front door where it can do its job, keeping my family safe from harm just like it did the night of the fire.

THE FIRE STORM

The fan above John's bed was churning the hot sticky air without giving any relief. The cottage never felt this uncomfortable before the death of his brother Jim. Grief seemed to amplify all the negative aspects of John's world. He let himself wallow in its depression.

The merciless heat had even turned the once vibrant vegetation of the forest brown as it too withered and died. Only the woeful call of the loons across the lake reminded him that this cottage was all that mattered in his life now. But he could not shake a foreboding, eeriness that something bad was about to occur.

Finally sleep took his sad old body to a place and time when he and his brother were young, strong and content. The dream took him away from the reality that nothing would ever be the same again.

"Uncle John, wake up. Something's wrong. I smell smoke and it sounds like someone is popping pop corn outside," Danny said roughly shaking his uncle awake.

John sprung out of bed. Billowing white smoke was curling up the slope of the roof in the open raftered living room. "Oh, my God. You get your brother and I'll get your Mom. We have to get out of here," he yelled. John picked up the telephone, but the line was dead. The reception on a cell was so bad at the cottage that he wouldn't waste his money on one of them.

Jane heard the commotion and realised immediately that the cottage was on fire, but not until the four of them stepped out in the night air did they see the wall of flames in the forest around them. They could not escape by the road. Their only chance would be to take the boat out on the lake and wait it out.

The heat was intense. Things were exploding in flames and tornados of hot air on fire, were swirling over the trees.

"Quickly get into the boat," John ordered rushing to untie the ropes form the dock. His heart was beating faster than he'd ever felt it beat before and there was tightness in his left arm. He paid no attention. He pulled the throttle rope and adjusted the gasoline intake, but nothing happened. Panic caused his hands to shake. On the second pull, the engine sputtered and whirled into action.

"Thank God you woke up when you did Danny and had enough sense to get me up too. We would have all lost our live in that," John said pointing back to the shore where flames now engulfed the cottage and the drive shed where the car was parked. Several explosions rang through the night as fuel tanks and combustibles caught fire. It looked like a scene from hell.

The twins were huddled together in fear and Jane, their mother was crying. This was the final straw in a long list of unforeseen circumstances and bad choices that had brought her to her father's and uncle's door.

John knew he had to do something to take away the heartache from his niece, so he started singing, "Oh we aint got a barrel of money, maybe we're ragged and funny, but we travel along singing a song, side by side."

That was Jane's Dad's favorite song. It was like a message from above. She reached over and hugged her uncle and joined in a chorus of the simple melody. The twins started singing along too.

The police boat rescued them and escorted them to the opposite side of the lake where they could dock safely. They heard that a lightning strike had started the fire. Later, in town, the Salvation Army took care of their immediate needs. The fire insurance would take care of the rest.

They were lucky to have gotten out of that fire storm alive. This was to be a new beginning for them all; one that re-evaluated and prioritized what really mattered; each other.

THE LIFE OF A TREE

A young seedling poked its head into the world, ignorant of the laws of nature. Its sole purpose was to stretch towards the sun, to gather strength from its warmth and unfurl its tender young shoots. In time those spindly shoots would grow into strong branches. Refreshed at night by the gathering dew and quenched by the falling rain, the seedling survived its first series of dry hot summers and freezing cold winters, to mature into a willowy sapling.

Nimbly the sapling's bows swayed, bending to the strong winds of life's wildest storms. Bravely, it spread its roots further into the nutrient rich earth for support, gathering strength and stamina. As the young tree matured following the laws of nature, the four seasons anointed it with their wisdom.

One pleasant spring day, buds appeared amongst its newly grown leaves, buds that developed into a profusion of lovely smelling blossoms. Honey bees, butterflies and other insects busied themselves pollenating the flowers. It was a glorious sight, arraigned in fragrant pedals, but alas they were not meant to stay. Soon the blossoms withered and fell to the ground.

      As the summer progressed, the tree's bows bent lower to the ground. Little green apples appeared and matured into bright red fruit. Deer arrived to eat the ones that hung on the lower branches or fell to the earth below. Some children came and climbed into the apple tree's canopy to pick the delicious fruit. Each apple held the seeds for another generation of its species, but very few would find the environment necessary to reproduce.

      After many years of growing fruit, age began to take its toll on the tree. Its trunk sported some gnarled- knots where branches had once grown. Its bark lost its smoothness and became more brittle, rendering it unable to bend to the wind, as it once had. Even the fruit it produced were no longer large or sweet. Eventually the sap that flowed through its veins slowed down and its branches became barren of leaves. The old apple tree was dying, but close to its weathered trunk a small seeding bravely pushed its head through the ground.

THE PRINCESS DRESS

I stopped to admire a stunning white brocade dress hanging in the window on a classy, ladies shop manikin. Christmas music greeted me as I pushed opened the heavy plate glass door and entered. The music, intended to enlighten shoppers to spend money in that establishment, had the reverse effect on me. It heightened my awareness of the ridiculous behaviour, I was engaged in. I never shopped in such high-end establishments, nor did I have money to spend on myself. I had many gifts for others still on my shopping list.

"You're wasting your time," the inner voice chided in my head. "And where would you ever wear a dress like that? Don't forget you have four kids to put winter boots on and you're not done Christmas shopping yet," it reminded me.

Just the same, I was drawn to that dress, like a moth to a flame. I found my size on the rack and headed to the dressing room. It fit like it was made just for me. I felt like a princess in it and the price tag affirmed it was meant to be worn by royalty.

Sadly, I slipped it off and brought myself back into reality as I redressed in my clearance rack clothes.

As I hung the exquisite garment back on the rack, I was startled by the voice of my sister--in-law's sister saying, "Hi Julie. That's a beautiful dress. We just received that shipment yesterday and there are only a few of them left. It would look great on you. Did you try it on?"

"I did, and it fits me perfectly, but I'm strapped for cash right now," I explained. I could tell from the expression on her face, she understood.

I had no idea she worked there. She even offered to buy it for me under her employee discount, but I assured her it wouldn't make any difference. As much as I loved the dress, unfortunately I could not buy it. "Maybe after Christmas", I uttered. I wished her a Merry Christmas and left the store feeling a little embarrassed about my sad state of finances.

Three weeks later it was Christmas morning. The children were delighted with their gifts and I was contented with the predictable gift of a flannel night gown and new slippers under the tree for me. I started tiding up the clutter when Fred, my husband got up from his chair and reached behind the chesterfield. He pulled out a rectangular foil wrapped box with a large red ribbon and bow on top.

"Santa must have dropped it behind the sofa," he teased to the children's delight" look it has Mom's name on it," he said handing it to me.

I knew he hadn't done the wrapping. It was a professional job. Surprised, I untied the ribbon and released the tape from the edge of the box. Delicate tissue paper covered the contents. Carefully I lifted the flimsy paper and there inside the wrapping was the beautiful white brocade dress I adored.

I squealed in delight, as if I was 10 years old. I held it up and danced around in circles like a jewelry box ballerina. I hugged my sweet husband and thanked him with a big kiss, but that was just the first of many times to come that he would be romantically rewarded for giving me such a special gift. Every time I wore it, I felt like a princess and fell in love with my prince charming all over again. Many magical evenings were inspired by that beautiful white brocade dress, for my prince charming and I.

ROLLER COASTER RIDE

Dressed in his Power Ranger t-shirt, camouflaged shorts, sneakers and a baseball cap, Harley walked on his tip toes past the height restriction line and through the turnstile of the world's wildest roller coaster. A roped off aisle inside the shelter, wove back and forth until it ended at the loading platform where a roller coaster train awaited its next load of enthusiastic passengers.

For Harley and his friend Kevin, this was their maiden voyage on the coaster known as the Python. They ran towards the front seat and climbed in. Harley flashed Kevin a nervous grin, wishing his heart would stop pounding in his ears. A loud speaker overhead blared out a warning to remove any hats, glasses' or lose items and put them inside your clothing.

Harley grabbed his cap and tucked it down the front of his shorts. The safety bar clanked down over their shoulders. Harley's mouth felt dry and the urge to pee nagged at him as his body stiffened and the coaster began to move with a jerk.

Slowly the chains beneath the roller coaster tightened, pulling the train of cars upwards towards the highest peak. Harley's teeth were tightly clenched. His hands gripped the bar in front of him so tightly that his knuckles turned white.

"Are you afraid?" Kevin asked.

"Na, not a bit," he lied. "How about you?"

"Just a little, I hope I don't throw up, that's all."

"Don't turn towards me if you do," Harley warned.

As passengers in the first car, they were allotted a few extra seconds at the top before the balance point was tipped and they would plunge into a wild death defying dive. Overlooking the straight down grade, Harley wished he could reverse his decision to ride this beast, but it was too late now.

Then it happened; with great momentum his body was lifted off the seat, jerked about and flung upside down as they were whipped around like a rocket ship on rails. Screams of terror filled the air. Harley's lungs were completely empty and somehow without consulting him first, his bladder was too. When the ride ended Harley was thoroughly embarrassed by the condition he and his cap were in. A huge wet stain covered the front of his shorts and urine dripped from his cap when he pulled it out of his pants. Trying to ignore the snickers from others nearby, he made his way down the off ramp with his hands in front of his soggy crotch.

Kevin found it funny too, but after his fit of giggles was under control, he became bent on helping his friend out of this embarrassing situation. "I know how to fix the problem. Follow me," Kevin said and Harley obeyed.

Harley kept his head bent down, walking a few steps behind Kevin's shoes and not making eye contact with anyone in the amusement park. When they stopped in front of a refreshment stand he tossed his favorite cap into the garbage can while his friend bought a pop. When Harley turned around, Kevin threw the contents of the paper cup into his face and all down the front of him.

"What the hell did you do that for?" Harley sputtered.

"Now it looks like you spilt pop all over yourself instead of pee."

"Oh. Ya! Thanks Kevin," Harley said looking down at his pop soaked shirt and shorts. They made their way to a washroom and Harley washed his hands and used some wet paper towels to wipe the pop from his face. In less than an hour his pants were dry and the day played out as if nothing out of the ordinary had happened.

    The boys couldn't wait to get home and brag to their friends about how much fun they had riding on the Python roller coaster for the first and for the last time in Harley's mind.

THE SHINY RED TOOL BOX

Looking into my five-year old's magical eyes I asked the leading question, "What do you want for Christmas, Bonnie?"

"A guitar, a drum and an organ," she immediately replied, letting me know she had given the matter a lot of thought.

We had four children, a five-year-old and three teenagers. Realistically, they were told not to ask for more than three items each, but Santa usually left an extra gift, or two, when he could afford to.

Images of my one girl, band began to throb in my head as I recalled the memories of her older sister's and brother's big band clamour when they were little. Somehow, I would survive Bonnie's musical onslaught too. Together we made and sent her Santa letter listing the instruments and inquiring about his and Mrs. Clause's health. It also spoke highly of how nice Bonnie had been all year.

With only a few days left before Christmas, my husband told Bonnie that he didn't want any clothes or slippers this year. He only wanted one present, a shiny red tool box, and furthermore he would like Santa to deliver it.

"Please Mom, write another letter and ask Santa to bring Daddy a tool box?" she begged, as we did the supper dishes together.

"But Bonnie, Santa can't bring presents for adults. He only comes to children, you know that." I replied, while thinking there was no way we could swing an expensive tool box, on top of everything else that needed to be looked after.

Her solemn expression showed deep thought, then her dark eyes sparkled, and her face lit up. "I know Mom; if I ask Santa to bring the tool box to me, instead of the guitar, do you think he might do it?"

The spirit of Christmas swept over me, as I stood there next to this loving child, who was willing to give up the gift she wanted most to make someone else happy. Sensing the love, I had for her, she gave my hand a squeeze before she fled from the room, returning with a pen, paper and envelope and another letter was written to Santa Claus.

Later that evening, after we went to bed, Fred and I discussed the situation and decided to honour our daughter's wishes and replace the guitar with the tool box. This was her sacrifice, her first Christmas to learn the joy of giving. It was not an easy decision to make. The guitar was destined to become her next birthday gift.

Christmas morning found all of us gathered around the tree, watching Bonnie scramble over the presents, looking for the biggest one she could find, and there on it was a tag that read, "To Bonnie, Love Always from Santa." Her brother helped her to maneuver it to her Dad's chair.

"Here Dad, I want you to open this present first," she said.

"But the card says it's for you," he replied, acting surprised.

"Yes. I know, but it's a special present I asked Santa to bring, so I could give it to you. At least I hope it's what I think it is," she queried, still a little unsure and crossing her fingers behind her back.

All eyes were on Bonnie and her Dad as they feverishly worked together to unwrap the package.

"He did it! He did it!, Bonnie squealed in delight, throwing her arms around her Daddy's neck.

''Well how about that," Fred uttered, while wiping the tear from his eye, before adding, "That's the best present ever!"

Not that he particularly meant the shiny red tool box inside the wrappings, but the Christmas spirit that the littlest member of our family brought to us. Through her generosity and love, she showed us the true meaning of Christmas.

"Are you sure you don't want to keep it and use it to hold your Barbie dolls?" Fred asked.

A funny look crossed her face as she contemplated his suggestion, but she decided not to take him up on his generous offer even though it had lots of little drawers to put her dolls shoes, clothes and accessories. She made the decision that the shiny red tool box, wasn't meant for Barbie dolls, it was meant to house tools. "It's ok Daddy.

You can keep it. I hope you like it, "she concluded.

    He picked her up and gave her a big hug as I wiped the tears of joy from my eyes. This was the best Christmas ever

THE THINGS I GAVE UP DURING MY LIFE

When I was a small child I waited for my father to arrive home from work, so he could swing me up onto his strong shoulders and carry me into the house. The world looked so different from his 6 ft. perspective. As time went by, my height and weight increased and my favourite way to enter our home had to be replaced with the more conventional one. That's about the same time as my petite mother decided I could use some lessons in gracefulness and poise. She enrolled me into ballet and gymnastics.

I was in an awkward stage of my life that I never completely outgrew. Like a gangly puppy, my feet had become too big for the rest of me and I kept falling off the balancing beam. As for ballet, I ask you, could you picture tall, chubby me in a tutu, leaping into the arms of some man in tights? Neither could I, so those dreams of being a prima donna ballerina were left by the way side, along with the ones of becoming a figure skater and circus, trapezes performer. A clown maybe; I do have the feet for it.

During my early teens, I gave up most of my childhood toys and stuffed animals, replacing them with collections of record albums and posters of the hit- parade or movie stars. This stage of my life was short lived; because, I became a wife and mother very young. I exchanged those carefree sock hop years for house work, diapers and potty training.

The whirl wind days of caring for preschoolers was replaced when they reached school age, by the balancing act of a working Mom. Juggling the family's needs with the demands of the work force meant putting aside any personal goals or dreams of going back to school. Just keeping some order in our home was a job that meant continuing to downsize the amount of stuff we accumulated. To lessen the chaos and clutter we got rid of any unused toys, furniture, or clothing, even if it held sentimental value.

Later as our children started leaving the nest to make their own way in the world, it became apparent to my husband Fred and I, that our role of parenting had also changed. Gone were the days of tucking them into bed, story-telling and putting band aids on skinned knees. Now they needed college tuition, cars, weddings and housing of their own. My husband and I somehow became their Free Finance Company. We had to learn how to let them be responsible adults and that wasn't always easy for me. I liked being a Mom and controlling the roost. What I did discover though, was the precious gift of time for me to indulge in taking night school and correspondent courses. I was 50 when I finally graduated high school and enrolled in some college level Creative Writing Course, but the biggest changes in my life were yet to come.

     They began when my husband died because of an automobile accident. I lost my best friend and business partner, that tragic day. At 55 years old I was out of work and in need of selling the century home on the 2 acres of land that had housed us and our trucking business for 30 odd years. It was all too much for me to handle on my own and the stress was taking its toll on my health, Sadly, I sold it all and started a new chapter in my life. The only thing I did promise myself was that I would be happy in the house I bought in Oshawa.

At first it was an act. I told everyone how much I liked it, how wonderful the neighbours were and how glad I was to be closer to the stores. The act soon became reality. I truly am happy in my new life. I have discovered things about myself like how I enjoy my quiet time devoted to writing and how the rest of my days can be spent doing the things I like, such as volunteering at the food bank and a nursing home. I have been fortunate to have made many new friends along the way.

My life has been a series of adapting to changes. No doubt there are more to come. I just hope I will be able to accept them as readily as I have so far. I realize now that even though I'll never be a ballerina, I can still dance; big feet and all.

THRIFT STORE PARKING LOT

Trudy drove her dilapidated old Volkswagen van to the local thrift store. She pulled up next to a shiny new BMW that looked out of place in that parking lot. As she stepped out of her van, the woman unloading the items from the classy sports car called her name.

"Trudy, is that you? What a nice surprise to run into you here. You're looking good," Jillian added, but she was wondering why Trudy always wore such trashy clothes. She was dressed in a skimpy pair of cu-t off short, shorts that were ragged around the edge and a Harley Davidson body shirt that showed off her well-endowed breasts.

"Are you still working at the Dainty Cafe?" Jillian asked her old co-worker, while noticing the dragon tattoo that Trudy recently had inked up her arm and over her shoulder.

"Yes. Not much has changed Jillian, since you left the café a couple of years ago. We were all so happy for you when you won the lottery," Trudy lied.

Jillian's appearance had improved over that time slot. Her once mousy brown hair was now blond with auburn streaks and her small chest had been enlarged to a double D. A face lift had reduced any wrinkles, but in Trudy's estimation, she still resembled a grey hound dog with her long thin face, but a rich one, with large diamond rings on every finger and a Gucci hand bag slung over her shoulder.

"What have you been up to?" Trudy asked, out of common courtesy.

"I have been busy getting my makeover. These cost me $10,000," Jillian proudly declared cupping both of her breasts right there in the parking lot. She had always been envious of Trudy's voluptuous figure.

"They look great," Trudy replied, while thinking, *if you were a cow*. "Where are you living now?" she inquired, knowing full well Jillian lived in a mansion on the rich side of town.

"Oh, I had my dream house built next to the golf course. It has a walk-in closet in the master suite that is larger than the trailer I used to live in. It is so full; I needed to get rid of some things, so here I am to donate them to charity," she smiled.

She would rather have sold her expensive items at a yard sale, but yard sales were taboo in her high-class neighbourhood.

"That's nice of you," Trudy said, wishing she had come to donate rather than shop. Trying not to lose face, she told herself, it didn't matter. Even if Jillian gave her discarded clothes to her, she *wouldn't feel right wearing them*, she thought to booster her pride.

Jillian never offered, instead she said, "You must come and see me sometime." But never gave Trudy her address. The last thing in the world she would want was Trudy showing up in her hippy bus or worse on the back of her boyfriend's motorcycle.

"Sure, sure I will," Trudy said. Adding as she walked away, "Stop by the Cafe and say hello sometime," all the while hoping that wouldn't happen.

"Yes, I will, if I can spare the time," Jillian lied. *When hell freezes over*, was her inner thought. She never wanted to be reminded of that greasy spoon, dive or the lowly position and pathetic pay she once received for waitressing there. Now her Country Club fees were more than she used to earn in a year, including tips.

Neither woman felt comfortable with the other any longer. The things they once had in common were no longer shared. Nor were they honest in relating their thoughts in their conversation. Both said one thing and meant another.

Life's like that sometimes for us all.

TRAILER PARK TACKY

  Something bizarre happened to me when I took up seasonal residency in a mobile trailer park, or camp ground, as we called it. Any sense of tasteful decor I may have once possessed became lost amongst the whirly-gig, wind-mills, gnomes, and plastic or wooden animal replicas that graced the lawn around my summer retreat. I even painted the rocks white that bordered the perimeter of our camp sight and thought they looked lovely.

  Campers are family orientated folk, who like to hang wooden signs at their entrance, with the names of everyone in their clan burnt into the wood. Other welcome signs adorning some trailers may reveal their poetic admiration with slogans such as, "If the trailer's a rockin, don't bother knockin."

  It's a red-necks life where patriotism runs rampant, with flags from many nations including the Jolly Rodger, and banners from every sports team known to man, flapping in the breeze. That same breeze carries along the tinkling of wind chimes, and the whine of country music flowing from a portable radio on a picnic table, or crackling from the outdoor speaker mounted in the tree.

In my park, flower beds add a blaze of colour to some of the most interesting planters. Some plants burst forth from the center of black rubber truck tires, or cascade from cut open rum barrels. Some clamour in confusion amid the bird baths, gnomes, Greek statues, fairies, and light house figurines. Many of the gardens produce an array of wild flowers also known as weeds. But, what would the garden be without the spiraling whimsy reflecting the suns bright rays, like a spinning tin foil masterpiece.

Campers can leisurely spend the hot hazy days of summer by playing a game of horse shoes or washer toss while staying cool drinking beer. If there is a boat for fishing, life becomes even more perfect. Meals served while in the camping mode are simple wholesome food like hot dogs, burgers and beans. And occasionally fresh fish caught on the lake. Often the food is served on throw away plates, to save having to wash dishes. No fuss, no mess.

When night falls and the lights come on, it's like Christmas has arrived in Toon-Town. Colourful light displays appear everywhere, from the potted fake tree on the patio to the umbrella hanging over the picnic table. On my camp sight, a flood light shines on three brightly painted, wooden butterflies attached to our shed. It also illuminates the clothes line that is constantly draped in damp towels and wet bathing suites. Some patio lights are handmade, out of empty bleach bottles trimmed with children's light bright lights. They are gallantly displayed on pillar and post. The store-bought patio sets drape every awning in Japanese lanterns, dragon flies and happy faces.

  At the end of each day, there is nothing more pleasurable than a blazing campfire, with folks dressed in baseball hats, lumber jack shirts, hoodies and jeans, circled around it, sitting on fold up lawn chairs, while drinking beer, swatting mosquitoes, choking on smoke and burning marshmallows.

  Yes! That is camping. Yes, it's tacky and yes, I loved every minute of it.

TWELVE MONTHS OF HEATHER

That tragic day when the March winds whirled,

When God sent his angels for our little girl.

April rains mingled with agony tears,

Heather was ours for ten short years.

May brought the blossoms, velvet and pink,

Her favorite colour, she wore on her cheeks.

June held its promise to love eternally.

How my heart warmed when she climbed on my knee.

July with its sky so hazy and blue,

Just like her eyes and the laughter they knew.

August, with golden wheat waving aloft,

The shade of her hair, so shiny and soft.

September when all the birds rejoice,

The memory of her sweet honey voice.

October colours as rich as wine,

Just as her memory remains on my mind.

November so crystal clear and bright,

It was her nature, so innocent and right.

December the month of holly and cheer,

But how our hearts ache with the loss of our dear.

January the promise of better and new,

We'll try to live the way she wanted us to.

February the days become darker it seems,

But our nights are aglow when she's in our dreams.

A year has passed with the coming of March,

But Heather will always live on in our hearts,

And the twelve months of Heather will ever more be,

A constant tribute to her loving memory.

UNMATCHED LUGGAGE

My travel plans for a Caribbean cruise in February, were made on a shoe string budget. An inside cabin and economy class flight awaited me and my family. I was anxious to experience my maiden voyage aboard a beautiful cruise liner, but the first adventure would be getting us to the airport.

Acknowledging that we were thriftier than the average Canadian tourist, we happily booked an American flight out of Buffalo, instead of Toronto to save a little money. On our departure date in February, a blinding snow storm arrived, but that never hindered our spirits.

Six of us made the trip crammed into a crew-cab, pick-up with our luggage covered by a tarp and a 10-inch blanket of snow, in the back of my son-in-law's truck by the time we arrived. The usual two-and-a-half-hour trip to Buffalo took five hours. We got to the airport terminal just in time for our plane to start taking on passengers.

Since the last time any of us flew on an airplane, a fee of $100 had been implemented on suitcases weighing above the allowed amount. My son-in-law's was over by several pounds. I found out why when he opened it on the busy terminal floor and started unpacking the cans of beer he had stashed amongst his clothing.

 To help him out, my daughter and I made room for some of his beer in our suitcases by removing the plastic shopping bags that contained our shoes and jamming them full of any items that could be brought on board the plane as a carry on. We then filled the empty spaces in our suit cases with beer cans and hoped our own luggage never weighed in above the restriction amount. It worked! Wally's favourite brew made the trip safely stored amongst our clothing, somewhere in the belly of the plane while our carryon luggage now sported labels from Walmart and Dollarama. This is how our holiday began.

 The fact that the cruise lines prohibited bringing alcohol on board never bothered these thirsty Canadians one bit. When I questioned the legality of it, I was told by my son that smuggling booze aboard goes on all the time, but when his suitcase never arrived in his stateroom, we began to suspect the worse.

Yes; his was one they inspected, and his beer was confiscated, to be returned to him on the last night of the cruise, he was informed. A farewell party was in the plans from that time forward.

No one in our group pre-booked excursions because, we were informed by others with previous experience, that it was much cheaper to arrange them with the island natives than on board the ship. During the seven days of island hopping, we took informative tours of sugar plantations and rum distilleries, shopped at several open-air markets, walked on white sand beaches, swam in turquoise, seas; saw towering volcanoes and lush tropical rain forests. Some of our group went snorkeling, some zip-lining, others swimming with stingrays and the non-modest folks, even investigated a nude beach, all at bargain prices.

At St. Maartens it was unanimously agreed upon to spend the day on the beach, where we were able to get a fantastic deal on the rental of a shade umbrella, a couple or lawn chairs and a bucket of beer, cheap! No transportation was needed because our ship was docked at the pier alongside the beach. It was time to lay back and enjoy a day on the shores of this tropical paradise without being rushed about.

      Austin, my nine-year-old grandson was with us. He took an avid interest in the native St. Martians who walked the beach selling hats, beach wraps and jewelry to the tourists. Austin could see an opportunity to make some money himself; by collecting sea shells and selling those to the patrons on the beach who had drank too many buckets of beer. As the day wore on, he filled his pockets with shells and coins while the adults lost count of the buckets and the shells they bought. Most of them made their way back on board somehow and tried in vain to act sober at dinner in the fancy, dining room with its Crystal chandeliers and white linen cloths.

      The ship was the most elegant I had ever seen. I was in awe of its beauty. The entertainment was top notch too. It boosted of an ice skating rink, a miniature golf course, a casino and three swimming pools. The only problem with the ship was that many of its 17 floors looked alike and the only way I could tell the front from the back of the ship was to look at the sea, to see which direction we were travelling. I was lost a great deal of the time and I should have taken off a few pounds, for walking I did trying to find my way around.

    The voyage ended with our private farewell party on the top deck, thanks to the returned beer. We all came home heavier than we left, but with lighter spirits, luggage and wallets. It was a great holiday, but the next time we fly somewhere, I will try to remember to bring along extra Dollarama bags, so our carryon luggage will at least all be matching.

VICTORIAN WAYS

Times were much different when my mother was a young girl. Etiquette, manners and the proper way for a young lady to behave, were top priority on my Grandmother Hettie's agenda for raising a daughter.

Keeping Marjorie dressed in freshly laundered and starched frocks, proved to be a massive challenge, due to her tom-boyish behaviour and dare-devil antics. Most days Hettie would change the child several times before the sun set. Besides doing her best to keep her daughter neat and tidy, Hettie was determined to teach her the proper etiquette rules to be a polite, well-mannered child.

Respecting your elders, neighbours and teachers, rated at the top of the list. It was considered improper for a child to ask anyone personal questions, or to talk back to an adult. The later punishable by the razor strap across the rump. The razor strap hung on a hook by the back door, as a reminder to behave oneself.

Once without realizing her breach of moral conduct, Marjorie told a neighbour's child that she thought the child's mother was going to have a baby. She had surmised this by the huge size of the woman's stomach. When her own mother's belly had swelled that large, she came home from school one day and found a baby brother in bed with her Mom. The neighbour child went home and reported what Marjorie had said. The very pregnant woman waddled straight over to Hettie's house and chastised her for allowing her daughter to talk about such things. Hettie was humiliated and Marjorie was made to apologize, even though she didn't understand why.

At 12 years old, Marjorie had no idea about the monthly cycle of the female body. She was utterly terrified when she discovered her under ware stained with blood. To make matters worse, her mother wasn't home and her father told her to stay in bed until she returned. Laying there for what seemed like hours, thinking she was bleeding to death, frightened her even more. When her mother arrived home and explained that this would occur every month because she was a girl and that it didn't happen to boys, she was outraged at how unfair that was. She was also told that she was now a young lady and as such should not speak about such things or kiss boys. No other explanation was given. End of sex education for her. The rest she would have to figure out on her own.

Etiquette and manners ruled every waking hour of Margie's childhood, but as she matured, she wondered why her parents had so many old fashioned ideas and rules to live by. Then she discovered that her mother, who came from Great Britain as a young girl, had been raised on an estate owned by Queen Victoria. Those true Victorian customs were brought over from England and upheld in her Canadian home as well

Thankfully Marjorie was too much of a rebel to enforce most of them onto me, her daughter, but having respect for others was taught and passed-down from one generation to the next. I am glad I don't live in the days of stays and corsets and the strict Victorian ways. But when I see the lack of respect many youngsters display today, I wonder if a razor strap hanging at the back door, might help correct some of their bad manners too.

WISDOM

In anticipation of reaching the age of wisdom, I have been thoroughly studying the subject. What has become clear to me is that wisdom is not the sage clever, perspective of those knowledgeable in the art of living, but rather the act of those skilled in camouflaging their inadequacies.

Wisdom is learning how to use your age to get out of doing the things you never wanted to do anyhow. It's finding pleasure in watching others tackle those unpleasant tasks and rewarding them with praise for being so strong, smart or kind, while you relax in your lazy-boy chair.

It's preventing yourself from being dragged into other people's affairs by saying wise words of wisdom like, "I have faith in your decisions", instead of giving them advice that can cast the blame on you when they screw-up.

It's calling everyone "dear" because you can't remember their names and asking for their opinion when you can't make up your mind, but then covering up your lack of certainty by pretending the direction of their response was the same course you intended to take in the first place.

It's learning how to answer a dumb question with a question of equal caliber, rather than look foolish by admitting your lack of knowledge or interest in the subject.

Wisdom is learning how to choose your debates more carefully by letting the ridiculous statements of others pass unchallenged, under the pretense of open-mindedness, while the truth that arguments upset the digestive system remains a secret.

It is learning how to do many things in moderation like: working, partying and making love. But when it's accomplished with the talented finesse called wisdom, it becomes a class act that takes years of practice to perfect. That's why people are usually older when they become wise enough to learn how to use it to their full advantage.

BIBLIOGRAPHY OF JULIE TAYLOR TIMMS

I was born on September 18, 1942, in East York on the eastern side of Toronto, to Marjorie and Harry Taylor. I was destined to be an only child for 15 years, until to my delight, my sister Wendy was born.

My fascination with words came early in my life. My Grandfather used to call me Mrs. Jones because I talked like a grown up from the time I started using the language.

We moved to Scarborough when I was in grade 5. I attended JG Workman public school. The excellent teachers I had there encouraged me to write and to enter the public speaking contests which I did. I was also the valedictorian on Graduation night even though my grades were not the highest.

I went to R H King Collegiate, but not for long before I left school, got married to Fred Timms and became a mother. By the age of twenty I had four of my five children. Writing was not on my radar screen except for a story or two I wrote for the children.

We moved to Oshawa in 1970 and started a trucking and excavation business called Timms Haulage and Backhoe service. Through reading the most boring books ever, I self-taught myself how to keep a set of books and became a partner in our business with my husband Fred.

In my late forty's I went back to night school and took some correspondent courses, to become a better writer. My spelling skills were always weak, so discovering the computer program that had spell check built in was a God send to me. I managed to talk my husband into buying a used one for me to write on. I took classes in Word Perfect to learn the program I most needed for writing and began to bring my elusive dream of writing into a reality..

After three years of taking courses I graduated from high school at 50 and took a couple of courses at Durham College to hone my writing skills.

As a senior, I joined the Oshawa Senior's Writers group and entered a contest held once a year through the library. My story took first place.

I was thrilled. The group has inspired me to continue writing.

I met a lady who wrote a children's story each year for her grandchildren and I decided to follow in her footsteps. My daughter Karen helps to bring the stories into print by working with the publishing company for me. Without her kind labours none of the eleven books I have written so far for children and for adults, would have made it to print.

Much of my inspiration comes from raising my five children and many grandchildren, from running our own business and from sharing my love of writing with others. I truly am blessed.

Manufactured by Amazon.ca
Bolton, ON